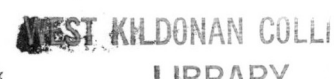 

$ 25.00

SPORTS SCANDALS

SPORTS SCANDALS
by Hank Nuwer

FRANKLIN WATTS
New York   Chicago   London   Toronto   Sydney

Photographs copyright ©: UPI/Bettmann Newsphotos: pp. 14, 17, 36, 61, 66, 88, 91, 102, 127; Wide World Photos: pp. 23, 68, 72, 74, 77, 80, 86, 96, 105, 113, 132, 143, 145, 149, 156, 164, 166; Gamma-Liaison, Inc.: pp. 29 (Michael J. Okoniewski), 52 (Barry King), 118 (Donna Zweis); Reuters/Bettmann Newsphotos: pp. 111, 158.

Library of Congress Cataloging-in-Publication Data

Nuwer, Hank.
Sports scandals / by Hank Nuwer.
p. cm.
Includes bibliographical references and index.
ISBN 0-531-11183-0
1. Sports—United States—Corrupt practices—Juvenile literature.
2. Athletes—United States—Attitudes—Juvenile literature.
I. Title.
GV718.2.U6N89   1994
796'.0973—dc20   93-26317   CIP   AC

Copyright © 1994 by Hank Nuwer
All rights reserved
Printed in the United States of America
6 5 4 3 2 1

For Bridget Klepeis, Joe Nikiel, Ken Oppenheim,
and Bob Waite

CONTENTS

INTRODUCTION
11

1
GAMBLING
15

2
RECRUITING
34

3
PERFORMANCE-ENHANCING DRUGS
51

4
ALCOHOL AND DRUG ABUSE
65

5
RACISM
85

6
SEX SCANDALS
104

7
CHEATING TO WIN
123

8
OUT-OF-CONTROL FANS
135

9
SUDDEN DEATH AND SERIOUS INJURIES
148

SOURCE NOTES
169

BIBLIOGRAPHY
183

INDEX
187

SPORTS SCANDALS

INTRODUCTION

The lives of athletes show us human nature at both its best and its worst. While it is natural for young fans to regard star players as heroes, it is important for them to realize that those blessed with great athletic skills are human and sometimes make mistakes.

Young people in particular need to come up with their own carefully thought-out personal definitions of precisely what constitutes a hero. Just because an athlete can throw a fastball 99 miles (158 km) per hour, complete a reverse dunk, or set a swimming speed record does not mean that he or she is worthy of emulation. Today's fans are infatuated with the world of sports. They wear team jerseys and caps. Their T-shirts, posters, and cereal boxes bear the likenesses of professional baseball, football, and basketball stars. Like the rest of society, their language contains many terms drawn from sports, and they devote much of their free time to watching professional sports.

Without question, sports heroes are given wonderful opportunities as a result of their media exposure, and some make the most of it. Former athletes such as Bill Bradley and Jack Kemp have used their popularity to go on to rewarding careers in politics, and other athletes find that their endorsements of presidential candidates are taken seriously by voters. Polls for most-admired Americans invariably include the names of several sports heroes.

This book does not say that all athletes are unworthy of emulation. However, it does give examples to show that fans should use greater discretion when choosing their heroes. Too often, as sportswriter Michael Roberts noted in his book *Fans!*, Americans use athletes as "human mirrors in which to see reflected themselves, with their collective qualities of nobility, morality and patriotism." Because sports promoters are only too happy to sell idealized images of athletes to the public, it becomes very important that fans learn to distinguish the real world from a commercialized dreamworld.

At the same time, seeing sports stars fail gives readers insight into the importance of allowing people a second chance. As this book makes clear, disgraced sports figures can often come back from a fall and begin their lives anew, vowing not to let their fans down again.

Many athletes say that they do not wish to be considered heroes. Many of them dislike giving autographs, toss away their fan mail unopened, and are openly disdainful of those who pay to see them play. This book reminds today's readers—who may be tomorrow's sporting heroes—that young people will be idolizing *them* someday. When the dreams of athletes become realities, responsibilities come with the territory.

This is not to say that all athletes are unworthy of being considered heroes. For every athlete who draws disgraceful headlines there is a player who tries to be a role model for fans. For every superstar sent to jail in disgrace, there are hundreds of fine athletes who give their time and money to civic groups and charities.

Sportswriters once protected sports figures. When the married Babe Ruth of the New York Yankees contracted a venereal disease, sportswriters covered up for him, blaming his illness on too much soda pop and too many hot dogs. Journalism, however, has changed. With so much money invested in sports, a newspaper's sports pages are taken very seriously. As a result, the Babe's excesses—if committed by a ballplayer today—would be scrutinized very carefully by the press.

Books on the scandalous side of sport are a necessary addition to every fan's library. The world of sports is a story not only of human accomplishments but of failures. The stories of those who have fallen from grace can be very powerful lessons for the rest of us.

Perhaps Bob Verdi, a columnist for the *Sporting News,* put it best when he defended two new books that depicted basketball player Michael Jordan and football coach Mike Ditka in a highly unfavorable light. "The greater the distance of sports heroes from us because of their high salaries and profiles, the greater our need to satisfy curiosities about who they really are."

—Hank Nuwer
Indianapolis, Indiana

Pete Rose holds the all-time major-league career record for hits. Yet he most likely will never be admitted to the Hall of Fame because of his involvement in gambling.

1

GAMBLING

Highlight films of Major League Baseball's greatest players would be incomplete without footage of Pete Rose, arguably the best hitter in the history of baseball. While playing from 1963 to 1986, Rose collected 4,256 hits, beating out the legendary Ty Cobb in the Most Career Hits category. But despite his on-the-field greatness, in his personal life he had a compulsive need to gamble on sporting events. And although nine of Rose's former friends and associates claimed that he bet on baseball games—including those he managed—he has strongly denied those accusations.

The job of investigating Rose was taken on by John M. Dowd, baseball's special counsel, working for baseball commissioner Bart Giamatti's office. Dowd took the testimony of more than forty witnesses, as well as a lengthy deposition from Rose. The investigator alleged that he had uncovered evidence showing that Pete Rose had bet on major league games, including those of his own Reds, from 1985 to 1987. One witness said that Rose bet as much as $20,000 a day on the outcome of baseball games.

A bookmaker claimed that he personally had taken more than $1 million from Rose in bets; another bookmaker said Rose owed him $400,000 for bets lost in just three months during 1987.[1]

The evidence that Rose bet on baseball was conclusive in then-commissioner Giamatti's eyes despite the ballplayer's denials. The investigation concluded in 1989, turning up betting slips signed by Rose. Once he had decided, the commissioner acted decisively. "Peter Edward Rose is hereby declared permanently ineligible in accordance with Major League Rule 21 and placed on the Ineligible List," said a document prepared by the commissioner.

"We are ridding baseball of a cancer," Giamatti added.

There was another aspect to the Pete Rose scandal—the death of Giamatti. Some sports commentators concluded that the stressful investigation had destroyed the health of the commissioner. Sportswriter Dave Kindred and commentator Howard Cosell blamed Rose, in print, for the commissioner's death.[2] Rose's supporters disagreed, citing Giamatti's long-time smoking addiction, an addiction the surgeon general of the United States has linked to heart disease.

One of the messiest parts of the national scandal was Rose's insistence that he did not have a gambling problem. Not until a judge sentenced him to jail for failing to report gambling income would he admit that he had an illness—compulsive gambling—that disrupts the lives of many ordinary people. Only then did he finally seek psychiatric help to cope with his compulsion to gamble.

Rose went to jail after he had pleaded guilty to two felony counts of filing false income tax returns in 1985 and 1987. U.S. District Judge Arthur Spie-

Rose's nemesis in the gambling scandal was baseball commissioner A. Bartlett Giamatti.

gel sentenced him to five months in prison, among other penalties and fines, for failing to declare income from card shows, gambling winnings, and the sale of Pete Rose memorabilia. Rose watched the 1990 World Series on a prison television.

Rose paid his debt to society, but his gambling addiction may have cost him his chance to be inducted into Baseball's Hall of Fame. If so, he will have been denied what he says was his fondest and oldest dream. "The ultimate goal to have as a ballplayer is to go to the Hall of Fame," Rose told *USA Today*. He said that he thought Major League Baseball would eventually allow him to be considered for induction, but he wasn't certain it would happen. "I'm not going to say I'm betting on it," said Rose.[3]

Rose's fight for reinstatement may take his entire lifetime. Certainly, he has many supporters as well as opponents. In his favor was the fact that when Rose agreed to be suspended by Giamatti, the commissioner conceded that Rose would neither confirm nor deny betting on baseball. Had Rose unequivocally said he had bet on baseball, his Hall of Fame chances would have ended at that moment.

In his book *What's Wrong with Sports,* sportscaster Howard Cosell said that Bart Giamatti will turn over in his grave if the ballplayer is inducted into the Hall of Fame. Commissioner Fay Vincent, who succeeded Giamatti and served until resigning in 1992, was opposed to Rose's induction. "The issue is really not just Pete Rose," Commissioner Vincent told *USA Today*. "The issue is baseball and what's best for baseball. . . . No one should kid themselves. Pete Rose bet on baseball. . . . None of the players permanently banned have been reinstated and there's a reason for that."[4]

Pete Rose was the fourteenth player suspended from baseball for gambling. However, many sports experts believe that certain other players have gambled over the years, but were lucky enough to get away with it. The first commissioner, Kenesaw Mountain Landis, appointed during the winter of 1920–21, suspected well-known players such as Tris Speaker, Ty Cobb, and Hal Chase of throwing games, but he lacked enough evidence to suspend them from the game. Investigators from the commissioner's office are far more sophisticated today about following up allegations, and they have the manpower and funds to finance thorough background checks. That was not true of Landis's investigations. In addition, because professional baseball was then in the process of trying to improve its image, it was to the commissioner's advantage to keep stars like Cobb and Speaker in the game. The public had already endured a major gambling scandal after the 1919 World Series, and Landis wanted the bad press to end.

Nonetheless, in retrospect many baseball historians claim that Hal Chase, in particular, threw many games during a fifteen-year career that lasted until 1919. He was a gifted hitter and fielder, but some of his managers and teammates believed he threw games on which he had bet. They maintain that he gave opponents runs by sometimes purposely missing balls thrown to him by other fielders. They charged that he was a genius at making these misplays look as if they were his teammates' fault, not his.

"He could do something like that and make it look so good," said former teammate Roger Peckinpaugh. "Any way you look at him, he was the greatest—the greatest first baseman and the greatest scoundrel."[5]

Chase was so slick a hitter and fielder that he was well loved by fans if not by his teammates. In that era, when sportswriters and ballplayers were the best of pals, and when sportswriters as often as not bet on games, few would print such accusations without concrete proof, such as signed betting slips. "Everybody knew it, everybody suspected it," said sportswriter Fred Lieb. "There were those who saw Chase associating with some of New York's most notorious gamblers, and it was common knowledge that he would bet against his own team. But he was just too popular a player for anyone to touch."[6]

But the gambling scandal involving members of the 1919 Chicago White Sox was eventually exposed by many newspapers, because rumors of player involvement were too numerous for the press to ignore. The so-called Black Sox, as the 1919 White Sox came to be known, did not merely throw a regular season game. They conspired to throw an American institution—the World Series.

The effect of the scandal was far-reaching. In those days, professional gamblers routinely attended ball games until individual clubs instituted policies to ban them. Many team owners, and even managers like John McGraw of the New York Giants, liked to gamble now and then.[7] But the Black Sox scandal made sports gambling taboo, and sports figures who gambled risked banishment from the game.

The 1919 Chicago White Sox were a great team and highly regarded by fans as a team that could easily defeat Cincinnati, their National League opponent. Some reporters suspected that all was not quite right immediately before the first series game, when gamblers began to place a lot of money on the Reds—even though Cincinnati had to face Chicago's nearly unbeatable twenty-nine-game-winning pitcher, Eddie Cicotte.

Cicotte was nearing the end of his career and was susceptible to taking money from gamblers, rationalizing that the Chicago owner had been underpaying him. He and seven teammates kicked the first series game away by a score of 9–1.

Those players not in on the fix for the White Sox played valiantly in the remaining games, but they could not make up for the intentional misplays of their teammates. The Reds won the World Series five games to three.

Nothing happened to Cicotte and his co-conspirators the winter after the World Series. But at the end of the next season, a Philadelphia newspaper reported a gambler's allegations that eight of the Sox players had deliberately lost games. One of the things that led to the downfall of the Chicago Eight was a boast by first baseman Hal Chase, a nonparticipant in the 1919 series, that he had won $40,000 betting on the series. The story was heard by many people in the baseball community.

Interestingly, many baseball historians say that a New York gambler and gangster named Arnold Rothstein had supposedly been the mastermind behind the thrown World Series. But he was too clever to leave a clear trail and was never convicted of a crime. Cicotte had made it known to two gamblers, Bill Maharg and "Sleepy" Bill Burns (an ex–big-league pitcher), that he and seven other Chicago players were willing to throw the series for $100,000. The players were naive enough to deal with the gamblers without taking cash in advance. As a result, most or all of the players failed to get the full amount they had been promised. Cicotte, for example, made $10,000, only a fraction of what he thought he would be paid.[8]

In the aftermath of the newspaper allegations, a grand jury was convened and Cicotte admitted to investigators that he had played to lose. The pitcher said he "grooved" his pitches to Cincinnati batters and played erratically in the field. He and seven teammates went on trial in 1921 for conspiracy, although the gamblers were not charged. Through some chicanery the confessions of Cicotte and the other players disappeared. Incredibly, as a result they were acquitted.

During the trial, Cicotte and superstar outfielder Shoeless Joe Jackson pointed fingers at their fellow conspirators—Swede Risberg, Fred McMullin, Buck Weaver, Happy Felsch, Claude Williams, and Chick Gandil. Cicotte named Gandil as the brains behind the gambling scheme.[9]

Significantly, the battle over Shoeless Joe Jackson's reputation continues to this day. When he first broke into baseball, the southern country boy played barefooted, hence his nickname. Unsophisticated and illiterate, he confessed to a crime he never fully understood, maintain his supporters, who nonetheless have failed in their bid to have Jackson admitted to the Baseball Hall of Fame. But without question, he remains one of the game's greatest hitters.

Stung by criticism, organized baseball instituted the office of commissioner, hiring Judge Kenesaw Mountain Landis and giving him authority to clean it up. Among his other acts, Landis banned all eight of the Black Sox. Although after the acquittal the players petitioned for reinstatement, Landis was unmoved by their pleas. The expulsions were for life. Not one of the so-called eight men out ever returned to organized baseball.

Until Pete Rose, the clear consequences of breaking baseball's rules against gambling made almost all players afraid to bet on games. Nonetheless, there have been occasional scandals. A later commissioner, A.B. "Happy" Chandler, suspended Brooklyn manager Leo Durocher in 1947 for con-

Judge Kenesaw Mountain Landis, in highbacked chair, presides over inquiry into the infamous "Black Sox" scandal of 1919. Judge Landis was made the first commissioner of baseball and charged with the task of repairing the game's tarnished reputation in the wake of the scandal.

sorting with known gamblers. Although Durocher was allowed back into the game, he has not been inducted into the Hall of Fame, even after his death, presumably because voters have concluded that his gambling had tainted his career.[10]

On occasion, professional football has also had gambling scandals. In 1963, Commissioner Pete Rozelle suspended two of the biggest stars of the era, Alex Karras of the Detroit Lions and Paul Hornung of the Green Bay Packers, for gambling on football games. Karras, later to become a successful television actor, was a defensive tackle without equal. Hornung, nicknamed the "Golden Boy" because of his blonde, youthful good looks, was Coach Vince Lombardi's star halfback during Green Bay's championship years. In addition, five Detroit players paid $2,000 fines for betting on the NFL championship game.[11] And the Detroit Lions franchise was fined $4,000.

The most publicized scandal involving the NFL occurred when Art Schlichter, a former Ohio State quarterback, detonated his professional football future by his compulsive gambling. He was suspended by the NFL in 1983 for gambling, but even if he hadn't been suspended, the Baltimore Colts would probably have dropped him from their roster. The young player had lost up to $1.5 million while gambling, and his on-the-field performances reflected his preoccupation with his debts. He lost up to $30,000 on a single bet. Although he entered a treatment program after bookmakers threatened to harm his family and break his throwing arm, his NFL career was over. He tried a comeback in 1987 with the Indianapolis Colts, but he immediately wagered some $230,000 on sports bets and again had to leave the game. In 1992, he reentered professional football as quarterback of the Arena Football League's Cincinnati Rockets, but he was arrested for writing a bad check and admitted that once again his gambling problem had overtaken him.[12]

Gambling problems have been a continuing problem in college athletics. One college football scandal occurred in 1989 at the University of Florida, when Gators quarterback Kyle Morris and other players were found to have placed sports bets with a Georgia bookie. Their scholarships were revoked, and they were suspended by the university. One fraternity mocked the whole situation. "Gator Football—You Can Bet on It," read a homecoming float sign.[13]

In addition to the University of Florida, four other schools—the University of Rhode Island, Bryant College (Rhode Island), the University of Texas, and the University of South Carolina—have been involved in gambling scandals in which athletes allegedly placed bets. In October of 1992, a Rhode Island grand jury indicted Bryant's basketball captain, Christopher Simmons, and former University of Rhode Island football player, Scott Kent, for their alleged role in a betting ring at their respective schools.[14]

In addition to these isolated incidents of college athletes betting on sports, there have been numerous times when players took bribes from gamblers to throw games or keep the score down. Point shaving, in which gamblers bet on the number of points that one team will beat another by, is the most visible problem.

College basketball is frequently the target of gamblers bent on making quick, illegal profits. One of the worst scandals to strike the sport occurred in 1949, and involved the vaunted University of Kentucky basketball program coached by Adolph Rupp, then a highly beloved grand old man of college sports.

25

In the opening game of the 1949 National Invitational Tournament, one of the greatest Kentucky teams of all time lost by eleven points to a mediocre Loyola team. For several months after the game, newspaper reporters and fans insinuated that the game had been fixed. Rupp insisted that this could not be so, saying that "gamblers couldn't get to our boys with a ten-foot pole." But if gambler Nick "the Greek" Englisis, a former Kentucky football player, couldn't persuade the players with a pole, he did persuade UK players Dale Barnstable, Alex Groza, and Ralph Beard to agree to play erratically in exchange for cash bribes.[15]

What the Kentucky players agreed to do was to make certain that their team's margin of victory was less than what professional gamblers believed the score should be. If gamblers thought a team should win by twenty points, that team's so-called point spread was twenty points. By mishandling the ball and deliberately missing some shots, dishonest players could alter the game's outcome but still win and ease their consciences. If the players did their part, the gamblers would win big wagers. Gamblers liked to bet on basketball because only five players were on the court at one time. One player pretending to have a bad game could have a major effect on the final score.

An investigation showed that the Kentucky players had cooperated with gamblers beginning on December 18, 1948, and had altered the score of several games, including the Loyola game. The plucky Loyola team played better than the Kentuckians had anticipated, and the points given away by the dishonest UK players caused Rupp's team to suffer an embarrassing loss.[16] Five Wildcat players, including three-time All-American Alex Groza, split only $2,000 for their cooperation.[17]

Kentucky was not the only college infiltrated by gamblers. Following a long, unpleasant investigation, some thirty-two players from seven colleges stood accused of altering point spreads. Those involved included stars from the City College of New York, winner of the 1950 NCAA and NIT national tournaments and the only team in history to win both prestigious tournaments. City College fired head coach Nat Holman, but rehired him two years later when an investigation proved he had no knowledge of gambler involvement with his team.[18]

Although the scandal damaged his reputation, Kentucky permitted Rupp to continue his coaching career. His status as a Kentucky legend made the university protect him despite ties to a bookmaker named Ed Curd. A Kentucky magistrate condemned both Rupp and the university, although he lacked the jurisdiction to take legal action against either. The president of the University of Kentucky, Herman L. Donovan, refused to fire Rupp, pronouncing him "an honorable man who did not knowingly violate the athletic rules."[19]

During the next decade, gamblers continued to approach young players and ask them to throw basketball games. In 1961, an investigation implicated twenty-seven colleges and fifty players in various gambling schemes. A co-conspirator in the basketball scandal, former college and NBA player Jack Molinas served five years in prison.[20]

In one of the most publicized of the 1961 scandals, the courts convicted three players from St. Joseph's for fixing games. Two of the players, team captain Jack Egan and center Vince Kempton, threw away promising basketball futures. Both had been selected to play in the NBA; the NBA banned the two for life. St. Joseph's forfeited a trophy for finishing third in the NCAA tournament.[21]

Although players were certainly aware of the consequences of throwing games, point-shaving scandals continue to rock college basketball. Seattle University players fixed games in 1965. Boston College players fixed games during the 1978–79 season, and one player drew a ten-year jail sentence for his cooperation with gamblers. After Tulane players fixed games in 1985, the New Orleans school discontinued the sport (although it has since reinstated it).[22]

In 1991, the University of Nevada at Las Vegas found itself under suspicion when the *Las Vegas Review Journal* published a photograph of three one-time Rebel basketball players in the company of gambler Richard Perry. Perry had been convicted in 1984 of attempting to fix games at Boston College. This incident embarrassed the UNLV administration and led to the resignation of veteran basketball coach Jerry Tarkanian. The situation degenerated into a mudslinging campaign between Tarkanian and Robert Maxon, the president of UNLV. Maxon, speaking during a Nevada State legislative committee hearing investigating the coach's resignation, said that Tarkanian supporters tried to retaliate by trying to "dig up dirt" on the university and on him [Maxon].[23]

Pro basketball has also occasionally become embroiled in gambling scandals. Jack Dolph, the first commissioner of the American Basketball Association, was a compulsive gambler.[24]

And a 1992 gambling scandal involved Michael Jordan, the Chicago Bulls high-flying superscorer. Newspapers reported that he had given $165,000 to golfing and poker acquaintances with very tarnished reputations. He later admitted the debt was for gambling losses, although he said he had not bet on basketball.

Superscorer Michael Jordan of the Chicago Bulls basketball team has confessed embarrassment at the bad publicity resulting from his gambling activities.

Jordan's misadventures began when he turned down an invitation to accompany his Chicago teammates to visit President George Bush at the White House in 1991. Bush aides had staged a reception to honor Chicago's NBA championship. Instead, Jordan made up an excuse for not attending and traveled to Hilton Head, South Carolina, where he played poker and bet on golf.

In December 1991, the *Charlotte Observer* broke the story of how Jordan gave a $57,000 check to golf pro James "Slim" Bouler, a man with a drug conviction being investigated by federal authorities for illegally disposing of money obtained in drug and gambling endeavors. Jordan said the $57,000 was a loan, but federal prosecutors disagreed, saying the check was for gambling debts. He later acknowledged that the prosecutors were correct. Jordan also wrote checks that totaled $108,000 to some other men—including bail bondsman Eddie Dow.[25]

At first, Jordan was defensive, saying "So what?" to reporters. However, he realized that gambling debts were a serious matter when the NBA began investigating him. The NBA cleared him of technical wrongdoing, but Jordan admitted that the bad publicity had embarrassed him, his family, and the Chicago Bulls.[26]

"As most role models or public people, you have to be very cautious of certain things that you do and the way it's going to be received and the perception of it," Jordan told *USA Today*. "I just wish that in all the negative things happening people can see me as human. I'm never out here to say, 'I'm perfect.' "[27]

A lawyer for the sports agency representing Jordan's many business interests said he hoped fans would accept his client's human errors. "Part of being a hero is dealing with success and the occasional failure," says David Falk of ProServe Basketball and

Football. "Mickey Mantle struck out. Johnny Unitas fumbled. There's got to be room in our adoration of heroes for the once in a while they strike out."[28]

Some sportswriters were less than forgiving. "Every professional athlete knows he has an obligation to avoid gamblers," wrote Dave Kindred, a columnist for the *Sporting News*. "To defend these stupid actions as your right is to be triply stupid."[29]

Halting gambling in sports is an almost impossible task in the United States. Americans spend more than $50 billion annually on illegal sports gambling, according to the FBI, and some $1.35 billion on legalized sports betting in Las Vegas alone. It is one of the country's most lucrative businesses. An estimated 50 percent of the illicit gambling in this country every year is related to sports.[30]

A survey in 1994 sponsored by the Commission on the Review of the National Policy Toward Gambling found that 61 percent of all Americans placed some type of bet. The practice is rooted in American history, which had horse racing even in the colony of Virginia. The commission also estimated that 5.5 million people illegally used bookies to place their sports bets. And somewhere between 1 and 9 million people in the United States may have a gambling problem, although the exact figure is difficult to determine because many people won't admit that they have a problem.[31] And gambling is such a common practice that some athletes joke about it. When third baseman Clete Boyer was fined $1,000 for gambling by then-baseball commissioner Bowie Kuhn, he said: "I'd go double or nothing with Bowie Kuhn, but I don't think he'd go for that."

Gambling has long been associated with sports events. Gamblers bet on the ancient Olympic games in Greece.[32] Many coaches say that it is hypocritical for the media to condemn athletes who gamble. They point out that the media contributes to the epidemic of gambling. College basketball coaches Bob Knight of Indiana and Dean Smith of North Carolina repeatedly tell reporters that when newspapers print odds they are sanctioning gambling. Many newspapers and television sports programs routinely give point spreads. Gamblers use this information to fill out betting slips. They also read the sports pages end to end, seeking information on injuries, player discontent, and player hot and cold streaks, so that they can better predict the outcomes of games. "I can't stand to look at a team that hasn't beaten the spread and thinks it's won," the late Pete Axthelm, an NFL TV sports commentator, once said.

The National Football League's security officers routinely keep abreast of Las Vegas wagering, knowing that they need to look into the possible fixing of a game if a point spread suddenly changes rapidly one way or another.[33]

Realizing that gambling is a problem, representatives from professional baseball, hockey, football, and basketball have lobbied in Congress to keep sports-sanctioned gambling from becoming legalized in states where it is now illegal. A Senate hearing on sports betting was greeted with the slogan "Don't Gamble with Our Children's Heroes" when representatives from the four sports met with the Senate committee in June of 1991. "We're all engaged in an effort to stamp this out," said then-Major League Baseball commissioner Fay Vincent.[34]

Nonetheless, professional sports have a tough fight ahead to win the war against gambling, especially since the interest of many fans would quickly fade if they could no longer bet on games, said James Ritchie, the executive director of the Commission on the Review of the National Policy Toward Gambling. "If all illegal gambling vanished, professional sports would rule the day," he said.[35]

So gambling scandals continue to make sports headlines. The coach of Indiana State, Tates Locke, who was himself involved in a recruiting scandal at Clemson University, aptly summed up the problem in his book, *Caught in the Net*. "If a school can buy the services of a player for a certain amount of money and promises, what makes you think a gambler out on the street can't also buy him?" he wrote.

2

RECRUITING

Recruiting scandals in America are as old as college sport. Even in the nineteenth century, some athletic departments visited rival institutions to steal talented athletes. Illegal recruiting escalated when college sports became popular during the 1890s and colleges began charging admission to football games.[1]

Today, the majority of National Collegiate Athletic Association (NCAA) recruiting violations occur in men's football and basketball programs, the programs most likely to attract lucrative TV contracts. The colleges that send basketball teams to the Final Four tournament receive more than $1 million each. Major football bowls pay winning colleges in excess of $2 million.

But even if profits weren't so huge, there would still be cheating. The addiction to winning is a powerful narcotic. Even the first college football game (between Rutgers and Princeton) had players in the lineup who had no right to be there. "At least one athlete, and probably three others, who could have been ruled academically ineligible" were participants in the game, which Rutgers won, 6–4, according to sportswriter Rick Telander.

The practice of wealthy alumni, who are commonly called "boosters," giving money to athletes in violation of accepted recruiting practices also goes back to the nineteenth century. By 1895, it had become a common practice for these "boosters" to pay the tuition and living expenses of prize college athletes.

In 1905, wealthy Milwaukee attorney Henry J. Killilea, impressed by a local sprinter named Archie Hahn, paid the youth's way to Killilea's alma mater, the University of Michigan. Killilea admitted that his conscience was eased when Hahn at least enrolled for classes. He looked down on the University of Nebraska, which had used non-students in varsity football games.

The University of Michigan frequently flaunted the rules in those early years of organized college athletics. For example, sports historians say that the school persuaded a professional baseball player from Montana, Tom Barry, to play illegally under the assumed name of Tom Bird. When opponents uncovered the deception, Barry went back to playing professional ball.

One of those responsible for fostering dishonesty in athletics at the University of Michigan was Fielding H. "Hurry-Up" Yost, the school's most successful football coach. Michigan reveres his memory at each home football game by adding one person to its attendance count; local legend has it that his spirit is there to support the Wolverines. At Michigan, he assembled 165 wins against only 29 losses and 10 ties in 25 years. His overall career coaching record for 29 years was 196–32–12, giving him an impressive .828 winning percentage. He fielded thirteen teams who enjoyed undefeated seasons.

Football coach Fielding H. "Hurry-Up" Yost was a legend in University of Michigan sports. He had a reputation, however, of doing anything and everything to win.

However, while Yost undoubtedly was a winner, his tactics were often criticized by educators of his era. Although the coach reformed his recruiting methods late in his career, for many years he beat the opposition by using highly unethical methods.

Prior to coming to the Ann Arbor, Michigan, campus, Yost cheated everywhere he coached. At Ohio Wesleyan in 1897, he paid four professional athletes to play for him. In 1898, while coaching at the University of Nebraska, he played two paid nonstudents to play against Kansas in the school's annual big game. Coaching at Stanford in 1900, he committed blatant recruiting violations.[2]

The University of Michigan knew about his reputation for pulling out all the stops to win, but because the school's alumni and students wanted a winner, the Wolverines hired Yost. Upon resigning from Stanford, he offered money to his most talented players if they would agree to accompany him to Ann Arbor, Michigan. Yost gave George "Dad" Gregory a salary of $1,500—big money in that era—to switch his allegiance to the Wolverines. At Stanford, Gregory had failed his classes, but Yost continued to play him, to the consternation of faculty members.

Among those Yost brought east from California was a top recruit, Willie Heston. The player accepted Yost's offer to put him on the Michigan payroll, unethically reneging on a commitment he had made to play football for Stanford. As a further incentive, Yost promised the player a job with the Wolverines team as an assistant coach when Heston's football career ended. Heston became one of the greatest football players of all time, scoring more than 100 touchdowns for the Wolverines, but he was paid for every point he scored. Heston was a professional playing with amateurs.

Yost invariably put football ahead of academics at Michigan. For example, he pressured professors to rule players academically eligible to play even when the grades of these students fell below minimum university standards.[3]

In 1905, Stanford president David S. Jordan condemned Yost's recruiting tactics. "Athletic fields should be closed for fumigation if we cannot prevent the use of money . . . in bringing in athletes to fill up the football team," he told *Collier's* magazine. "I know that the professors of Michigan have been quite alert to the injury which the victories of Mr. Yost have caused to the reputation of Michigan."

Yost never lacked for strategies to keep his star players happy and well paid. He smoked stogies in public and allowed a tobacco company to manufacture cigars that bore his name, sharing the profits with three of his best Michigan athletes.

The coach persuaded wealthy alumni to unfairly favor athletes over other students. The alumni gave players jobs at salaries far higher than the work was worth. Some players did little or no work, but the employers still paid them.[4]

In recent years, colleges have been no less deceitful. At any given time, the NCAA lists more than two dozen colleges on probation for recruiting violations. Typical of such violations is a scandal that occurred during University of Kentucky basketball coach Joe B. Hall's career—a thirteen-year reign that saw his teams win 297 games against only 100 losses, including an NCAA championship and three Final Four appearances.

A Pulitzer Prize–winning investigation by the *Lexington Herald-Leader* revealed that many players joined Hall's winning teams because UK had been the highest bidder. The newspaper said that college boosters gave players under-the-table payments as high as $4,000, and that they paid as much as $1,000 for free season tickets held by the players.[5]

Although a flurry of denials issued from those connected with the University of Kentucky program, thirty-one of thirty-three players interviewed by the newspaper admitted that they knew of recruiting infractions at UK that were illegal under NCAA rules; another twenty-six players said they themselves had knowingly broken the rules. Kentucky star Kyle Macy, later a standout NBA performer, said that boosters slipped him illegal cash gifts while shaking hands. Player Jay Shidler alleged that he received $8,400 from Hall's attorney in exchange for his complimentary tickets, a clear violation of NCAA rules, if true. All-American Sam Bowie said he was paid up to $500 a talk for addressing groups of Kentucky fans, another violation.[6]

Although Joe B. Hall insisted that he was "personally unaware of any NCAA rules being violated," *Herald-Leader* reporter Jeffrey Marx argued otherwise. "There was a wide range of what the players thought Hall's involvement was, anywhere from 'he knew what was going on,' 'he didn't know what was going on,' 'he didn't want to know what was going on,' 'he knew but looked the other way,' " charged Marx.[7]

When the scandal broke, not surprisingly, *Herald-Leader* readers were irate. Instead of venting their rage on the Kentucky program, they attacked the reporters who broke the story. "I had no idea the extent to which it would become a problem in my life," said Marx. "There were things like death threats and a bomb scare at the paper."[8]

The attitude of Kentucky players toward play-for-pay college basketball was summed up by Kevin

Grevey, a UK forward who played from 1972 to 1975. "I personally say, the more the merrier. If a kid can get this or that, take it."[9]

Many colleges continue to commit recruiting violations even when coaches leave or are replaced. Certain practices apparently die hard. For example, after Hall retired from the University of Kentucky, the school nonetheless had another recruiting scandal during the 1988–89 season. Among other things, Kentucky recruit Chris Mills allegedly received a $1,000 cash payment delivered by overnight mail—a charge Mills and his father deny. The scandal resulted in the resignation of Hall's successor, head coach Eddie Sutton, now the basketball coach at Oklahoma State University.

Kentucky is only one of many repeat violators. Other collegiate athletic programs that have committed multiple NCAA recruiting violations include programs at Clemson University, Southern Methodist University (SMU), the University of Florida, the University of Illinois, Wichita State, Tulane University, Memphis State, the University of Oklahoma, Syracuse, Southern California, the University of Texas, the University of South Carolina, Texas Christian University, and Oklahoma State University. All of these institutions were involved in more than one scandal, committing serious recruiting improprieties in recent years.

One program that reformed itself in recent years is Southern Methodist University, but not before the school came to the attention of the NCAA. In its heyday as a football power, the school paid top athletes to play football. In 1987, the NCAA hit the Mustangs with the so-called death penalty, leveled because the school was found guilty of two major violations within a five-year period. (Other colleges to receive the "death penalty" were the University of Kentucky [1952–53] and Southwestern Louisiana [1973–75] for multiple recruiting violations in their basketball programs.)

Among other improprieties, SMU boosters improperly paid $11,000 to recruit Sean Stopperich. Coaches drew $61,000 from an illegal fund to pay thirteen football players. Then Texas governor Bill Clements, an SMU trustee, admitted that he had known about payoffs and agreed to remain silent about them so that the university wouldn't be embarrassed.

As with most NCAA investigations into recruiting violations, those SMU players who had taken illegal payments were not punished for their actions. Because most players receive immunity from the NCAA in exchange for their testimony against their schools, they are free to transfer to other NCAA institutions. Many honest SMU players with no knowledge of the payoffs were devastated that their peers had been on the take. "I was shocked when I heard it," said SMU tackle David Bryan.[10]

It occasionally happens that a coach goes unpunished from leaving a program that the NCAA has punished. When a scandal occurred at Clemson during the late eighties, football coach Danny Ford accepted a million-dollar buyout of his contract even as the NCAA was getting ready to penalize the Tigers for violations committed under him.

Other coaches escape punishment because recruiting violations are revealed only after they have left their programs. Former Auburn basketball player, Chuck Person, now an NBA player, waited until his coach, Sonny Smith, had left the team before admitting that two boosters and alumni gave him cash payments in violation of NCAA rules.[11]

An investigation into one aspect of an athletic program may expose unethical practices in another. During an investigation into point shaving at Tulane University, it was learned that the basketball assistant coach had also committed many recruiting improprieties. For example, the staff had paid "Hot Rod" Williams, a star basketball player with a subpar high school academic record, an inducement of $10,000 to influence his choice of school.[12]

Coaches will also try to gain an edge by breaking the rules to pay extra money to their assistant coaches as a performance bonus. When it was revealed that University of Florida football coach Galen Hall had paid two assistants unethically from a private fund, he left Gainesville surrounded by scandal. He had broken his promise to run a clean program after taking over the team from his coaching predecessor, Charley Pell, whom the NCAA had also judged guilty of committing serious recruiting violations.

While many coaches, college trustees, boosters, and athletes are honest, many do flaunt NCAA rules. Rarely does a basketball or football season pass without several colleges being put on probation. With the integrity of major college sports called into question, the Carnegie Foundation for the Advancement of Teaching suggests that colleges should lose their accreditation status when they commit recruiting violations. "Big-time sports are out of control," lamented Ernest L. Boyer of the Carnegie Foundation, advocating strict punishment for those who fail to comply with NCAA rules.

One of the practices condemned by Boyer is that of too many colleges willingly abandoning standards for admission. So-called blue-chip prospects are admitted in spite of their unsatisfactory high school grades and results on standardized tests. But some educators say that too much attention is given to these tests. For example, the NCAA requires incoming freshmen athletes to achieve minimum SAT (Scholastic Aptitude Test) scores or be ruled ineligible to play their freshman seasons. The objection of many educators to this is that such standardized tests discriminate against poor or minority athletes. They maintain that the tests particularly discriminate against students of color. The director of athletics at Georgetown University, Frank Rienzo, has called the tests "discriminatory," arguing that grade-point averages are a more reliable way to predict which athletes have the wherewithall to succeed in college.[13]

NCAA studies show that the tightened Proposition 48 rules from 1986 to 1992 have had both good and bad results. The bad news is that the rule disproportionately made black athletes ineligible for Division I (major college) sports. The good news is that the number of black athletes ineligible in 1991–92 was slightly less (4 percent) than the number ineligible in 1990–91, which might mean that high schools are better preparing athletes for the aptitude tests.[14]

Nonetheless, the low graduation rate of black athletes continues to concern educators. Only a quarter of all black athletes graduate. Many of those who do earn a diploma have been encouraged by the coaching staff to take unchallenging majors, or majors in some aspect of athletics, to protect their eligibility by keeping their grade-point averages up. In the former case, the players too often graduate without the educational background for a good job. In the latter case, graduates in athletics far outnumber the job vacancies. Coaches tell athletic department advisers to "cluster" marginal and less than marginal student athletes in easy, so-called Mickey Mouse majors, majors that are never in demand by employers. In 1987, three Indiana University researchers found that nearly two-thirds of Division I programs clustered athletes in what the *Sporting News* called "all-but-bogus" degree programs.

Another concern is that some colleges admit athletes who have high school grades and aptitude test scores that are much lower than those of the nonathletes accepted to the same schools. While some schools such as Duke University and Notre Dame continue to call for high academic standards for athletes, other schools fight to relax standards. In contrast to Duke and Notre Dame, University of Miami head football coach Dennis Erickson blasted the NCAA's decision to raise minimum high school grade-point averages from 2.0 to 2.5.

The University of Miami is a good example of what can happen when less than stellar student athletes find themselves competing academically against far brighter and better-prepared classmates. Miami has spent large sums of money to recruit academically gifted students; these students invariably achieve grades far superior to students on the championship football team, and many athletes have had trouble achieving even the minimum acceptable grade-point average. Former Miami coach Jimmy Johnson recruited students who lacked the preparation and abilities needed for college. In 1987, at least six members of the team had verbal SAT scores of 270 or lower. One starting player had a verbal score of 200, the score given just for showing up.[15]

The pressure on these athletes at Miami has been tremendous, particularly given the demands of their coaches.

As an example of what this pressure can do to a college athlete, *Sports Illustrated* reported that a tight end for Miami took eighteen Tylenol tablets in a suicide attempt. The young man admitted that he simply lacked the academic expertise to cope with the academic and disciplinary demands of college.[16]

To try to compete, athletes at some colleges have resorted to cheating. The University of Arkansas suspended Todd Day, a star basketball player, after he had received answers in advance to a test.[17] A University of Miami academic counselor resigned because of wholesale academic cheating by the football team. "Cheating seemed to be endemic on the campus when I was there," claimed the counselor, Alan Beals.[18]

Players have also been caught cheating to get *into* college. One case of alleged academic fraud occurred at the University of Kentucky in 1987, while Eddie Sutton was coach. The NCAA charged that Wildcats star Eric Manuel, fearful of becoming a freshman eligibility casualty, had cheated on his American College Testing (ACT) examination, one of two standardized tests all college recruits must take to be considered for college admission.

Although Manuel denied the allegations, an NCAA investigation determined that the results of his ACT test were highly suspicious. Of 219 answers on Manuel's test 211 exactly matched the test answers of a student who had sat to his immediate left. ACT officials said there was a two-in-a-million chance of two people handing in the same score.[19] Manuel's ACT test score was twenty-three, well over the NCAA Proposition 48 requirements, while his two previous college entrance tests had ACT equivalents of three and seven. Improvement like that was almost statistically impossible, said ACT officials.[20]

But while the NCAA was never able to prove whether Manuel cheated, or whether someone with

UK loyalties played fast and loose with the ACT test, it chose to punish only him. Although the Kentucky coaching staff had much to gain if Manuel passed, the NCAA put all of the burden of responsibility on the player. It banned Manuel for life from NCAA play.

In the aftermath of the Manuel case, critics charged racism on the part of the NCAA. The governing body convicted Manuel, a black player, while Sean Sutton, a white UK player and son of the coach, was allowed to become eligible to play at Oklahoma State University, where his father had taken a new coaching job. Sean Sutton had admitted lying to the NCAA investigators, and critics thought he should receive penalties as severe as those dealt Manuel.

Charges of exploitation of black recruits have been leveled many times by the press. White athletes in 1991 graduated twice (52.2 to 26.6 percent) as often as black athletes, said an NCAA study released in 1991. Many more black athletes than white players dropped out of college in their fourth or fifth year of study, because school advisers had told blacks to take easier subjects that would keep them in school until their eligibility expired, said Richard Lapchick of Northeastern University's Center for the Study of Sport in Society. As a result, the black students had to pass their hardest requirements when they were no longer of use to their coaches and no longer (in some cases) had tutors paid by the athletic department available to them.[21]

In 1991, a black athlete at Ohio State charged that his coaches insisted that his academic pursuits had to take a backseat to athletics. Premed student Robert Smith quit the Buckeye football team for one year, saying that his coaches had done everything possible to interfere with his studies. They ordered him to miss classes in order to attend practice. One assistant head coach told him flatly that "You're here to play football," and "You take school too seriously."[22]

The most publicized recruiting scandal occurred in 1986. Jan Kemp, coordinator of the English section of the University of Georgia's Developmental Studies Program, took her employers to court, charging that they had committed academic fraud to keep new recruits eligible.

Demoted and then dismissed by the university after blowing the whistle on the school's preferential treatment of athletes, Kemp won $2.6 million when a jury believed her rather than University of Georgia officials.

Her testimony charged that Georgia administrators put winning above nearly everything else. Particularly damaging was a secretly taped admission, made by the administrator who fired Kemp, that Georgia exploited black recruits.

"I know for a fact that these kids would not be here if it were not for their utility to the institution," said Leroy Ervin, a black administrator, on the tape. "There is no real, sound academic reason for their being here other than to be utilized to produce income. They are used as a kind of raw material in the production of some goods to be sold . . . and they get nothing in return. . . ."[23]

Adding to the scandal, Kemp proved in court that, among other things, football players who failed English were given special treatment to keep them eligible for the Sugar Bowl. In addition, she demonstrated that the school recruited and admitted all but illiterate students as long as they displayed exceptional athletic ability.[24]

Another disappointing story about American education and athletes broke in 1991. Female athletes in some American colleges have had as difficult a time as male athletes in securing a diploma. San Diego State admitted that it had graduated only one of twelve recruits in five years. Eastern Michigan (two of twenty-one), Montana (three of eighteen), Colorado (three of sixteen), and Louisiana State (four of sixteen) also had dismal graduation rates for athletes.[25]

In August 1992, the NCAA published a "Graduation-Rate Report" for male athletes that embarrassed many major colleges. A total of 198 basketball programs out of 297 colleges in the survey failed to achieve a graduation rate of at least 51 percent. Moreover, 31 of the 198—including such well-known schools as the universities of Houston, Texas–El Paso and Alabama—failed to graduate a single player who entered their schools in 1983 and 1984. In contrast, fourteen colleges listed 100 percent graduation rates for basketball; one of the schools was Duke University, winner of the NCAA Tournament in 1992.[26]

The 1992 results also show that black players are graduating in insufficient numbers. Only 20 percent of black players graduated.[27]

One player who claimed his school exploited him was Kevin Ross, a starting basketball player at Creighton University. After leaving the school, he found that he couldn't get a job because he had never learned how to read. Yet not only did Creighton admit him, but he managed to pass several college classes even though he was functionally illiterate. Ross and Creighton recently settled an exploitation suit in which the former player received a settlement, but the school did not have to admit it had been at fault.

After the Ross scandal, professional football player Dexter Manley confessed that he too had passed his classes at Oklahoma State despite his inability to read.

Few people in major college sports escape recruiting violations. That lesson was made public in April 1992, when NCAA executive director Dick Schultz said that he "should have known" about apparently improper interest-free loans to University of Virginia athletes while he was the school's athletic director from 1981 to 1987. Schultz and other athletic administrators were guilty of "neglect" and "insufficient knowledge of the [NCAA] rules," said UV president John Casteen.

Although Schultz first said that he had no plans to resign, saying that he had known of no wrongdoing, he eventually quit because his effectiveness as an administrator was being called into question. The scandal further eroded public confidence in college sports and the NCAA's ability to control violations.[28]

Another difficulty for the NCAA in regulating recruiting is the fact that many universities see nothing wrong with hiring coaches who have left other colleges following recruiting scandals. Even coaches with two or more recruiting scandals in their past find employment as long as university employers think these coaches can build winning programs.

Coach and athletic director Jackie Sherrill left Texas A & M following the NCAA's condemnation of multiple recruiting infractions. A & M committed twenty-five violations, drawing probation for two years. "I never told you that we were pure," said Sherrill, admitting guilt in some of the infractions.

Mississippi State overlooked Sherrill's problems at A & M, as well as some allegations that had surfaced previously when the coach worked at the University of Pittsburgh. State's president Donald

Zacharias said, "I feel comfortable with the decision" to hire Sherrill.[29]

On a positive note, some schools always recruit on the up and up. For example, Rice University in Texas has never been accused of offering illegal inducements to recruits. "At Rice they're looking for the student-athlete, not just the athlete," former Rice tight end Kenny Major said. "I never felt like a piece of beef with a meat hook in my side."[30]

3

PERFORMANCE-ENHANCING DRUGS

On May 14, 1992, a headline sports story frightened many users of performance-enhancing drugs in gyms and locker rooms across America. On that day, the once-invincible former football star of the Oakland Raiders, Lyle Alzado, died from brain cancer. Because he had been variously an NBC sports commentator, an actor, and had tried a comeback that failed in 1990, Alzado was a celebrity. His death created shock waves because in the months before he died he admitted that he had used anabolic steroids, a synthetic derivative of a male sex hormone used by some athletes to build more powerful physiques and enhance performances on the field.

In the months prior to his death, Alzado added that not only had he used steroids while playing football in college and the NFL, but that he had continued taking them after his retirement. "Mr. Alzado . . . is a good [negative] example . . . because he never quit using that drug," said a steroids expert, Penn State professor Charles Yesalis. "He admitted he just couldn't live without it. . . . Those drugs can create psychological dependency."[1]

Former professional football player Lyle Alzado, shown here with his wife, admitted shortly before his death from brain cancer in 1992 that during his playing career he had made extensive use of performance-enhancing drugs. It is unlikely, however, that those drugs caused his terminal illness.

Alzado believed that the drug had caused his brain cancer, but Yesalis discounted that possibility. Nonetheless, Yesalis emphasized that the use of steroids has been linked with other serious health consequences. Athletes risk becoming ill with hepatitis or dying of AIDS through sharing dirty needles. They can suffer depression and acquire suicidal tendencies from withdrawal. Other possible consequences include shriveled male gonads, muscle tears, high blood pressure, stunted growth in teenagers, clogging of the arteries, manic behavior, masculinization of women, and impaired kidney and liver function.

Because anabolic steroids often enhance strength, speed, and athletic performance, many amateur and professional athletes have taken them despite the dangers. When these athletes fail drug tests and are exposed, the scandals can have devastating emotional consequences. After the NFL barred player Terry Long for using steroids, the distraught player attempted suicide.

Because Alzado was far better known to the general public than Long had been, his story had more impact. After being diagnosed with inoperable brain cancer in 1991, Alzado admitted that he had spent up to $30,000 annually for performance-enhancing drugs and human-growth hormones while playing variously for the Oakland [now Los Angeles] Raiders, Denver Broncos, and Cleveland Browns.

The Alzado case cast doubt on the statements of many NFL players that they were free of steroid use. All through his professional career, Alzado repeatedly denied that he had a physical edge from taking steroids. "I lied to a lot of people for a lot of years when I said I didn't use steroids," Alzado told *Sports Illustrated,* noting that in his prime the drug had boosted his weight from 190 (86 kg) to a muscular 300 pounds (136 kg).

He charged that steroid use in the NFL is far greater than many people believe, and that the NFL for too long covered up the extent of the problem from the public. He noted that the league failed to insist on testing for performance-enhancing drugs until 1990. "Ninety percent of the athletes I know are on the stuff," said Alzado in 1991, a scarf on his head to hide his baldness caused by chemotherapy. "We're not born to be 280 or 300 pounds [127 or 136 kg] or jump 30 feet [9 m]. Some people are born that way, but not many, and there are some 1,400 guys in the NFL."[2]

The Alzado story is only one of several scandals involving performance-enhancing drugs. In fact, worldwide steroid scandals have become so commonplace that these stories wind up on the front page of the sports section only when big-name athletes are involved.

An explanation of why some athletes take such risks with their health was given by actor and bodybuilder Arnold Schwarzenegger in a *U.S. News & World Report* interview. Admitting publicly that he too had taken small dosages of steroids for a time, Schwarzenegger said "We are in a very fast world now, and we're always looking for a shortcut. We always want to get rich the fastest way, we want to get famous the fastest way, we want to get strong and be competitive the fastest way."

But Schwarzenegger said that those who think steroids are worth the risks involved are mistaken. "It was not the drug that made me the champion," he said. "It was the will and the drive and the five hours of working out, lifting 50, 60 tons of weights a day, being on a strict diet and training . . . that I had to do."

Schwarzenegger's use of steroids occurred more than twenty years ago. Many steroid users are unaware that the use of steroids goes back to the 1930s. Medical researchers first administered the drug to aging men to try to build strength. Because steroids were commonly used to fatten cattle, in 1956 the Soviets felt there would be no harm in giving testosterone, the male sex hormone, to Olympic athletes of both sexes. When athletes from other nations, including the United States, detected that the steroids were giving the Soviets an edge in events such as wrestling and weight lifting, they too began taking them. In particular, the East German sports authorities sanctioned the regular practice of giving performance-enhancing drugs to that country's male and female athletes during the 1970s and 1980s, enabling the East Germans to dominate sports such as women's swimming. It wasn't until 1989 that all nations agreed steroids were a serious enough problem to ban them; the Soviets and the United States signed a joint drug-testing agreement that year.

But in spite of such progress, experts believe that steroid use has increased, conservatively estimating that as many as 1 million people may take them.[3]

Another former NFL player who blames steroids, in combination with heavy drinking, for a life-threatening condition is Steve Courson, a nine-year veteran with Pittsburgh and Tampa Bay. Courson, who was once one of the strongest men in pro football, now has a potentially fatal heart problem that exhausts him if he does something as routine as climb a flight of stairs.[4]

Courson's highly publicized admission gave the public a wake-up call with regard to the extent of steroid use among college and professional football players. He admitted taking doses of steroids that were as much as ten times what the manufacturers had recommended.

Public attention focused on the abuse of steroids in the NFL when a U.S. Senate Judiciary Committee launched an investigation of steroid use in 1989. Atlanta Falcon guard Bill Fralic charged that three-quarters of all NFL linemen, linebackers, and guards had used steroids to build their bodies artificially. He admitted that he began taking drugs as a freshman at the University of Pittsburgh.[5]

Since the NFL requirement for steroid testing has been instituted, the number of pro football players caught taking performance-enhancing drugs has dropped. Nonetheless, some players continue to risk their careers for gains in strength and performance. Terry Long, mentioned previously, a starting guard for the Pittsburgh Steelers for six and a half seasons, tested positive for steroids in July 1991.[6]

Some experts maintain that the lower number of players apprehended is misleading. They say that many football players haven't gotten cleaner—they've gotten trickier—and that steroid use is much higher than the NFL would like the press to think. The former NFL drug adviser, Dr. Forest Tennant, told *USA Today* that up to 20 percent of all NFL players continue to use steroids.

What the players are doing to avoid detection, reveals Tennant, is to take water-soluble steroids that leave the body more quickly than other steroids. In this way, steroid users can defeat the drug test. A few athletes use human growth hormones (HGH), which don't set off an alarm when users are tested for steroids. Nonetheless, HGH can also cause potentially dangerous side effects similar to those experienced by steroid users.[7]

Many college football players have used steroids. When football star Brian Bosworth of the University of Oklahoma, an outspoken critic of street drug use, tested positive for steroids in 1986 and was declared ineligible for a bowl, he tried to downplay the news that shocked his many young fans. "I'll continue to fight against the abuse of drugs—recreational drugs that are destroying society," he said during a press conference. "Steroids aren't destroying society."

Bosworth was one of the twenty-one players the NCAA caught taking illicit performance-enhancing drugs in 1986. Steroid use continues to plague college football. Following the passage of the Anabolic Steroids Act in 1991, the federal Drug Enforcement Administration arrested thirty-two people in Phoenix, including Arizona State University redshirt football player Robert W. "Bill" Doverspike. The player claimed he had sold steroids to teammates, although an ASU spokesman countered the claim, saying that he didn't feel steroids were a problem with his athletes.[8]

Many players on a single college football team may use steroids. During the mid-1980s, when then coach Jimmy Johnson's University of Miami Hurricanes vied for a national title, *Sports Illustrated* alleged that some players had taken steroids to gain an edge.

Sources told the magazine that as many as two-thirds of the Hurricane football team were steroid users. "You'd come in and find syringes in the corner of the locker room," ex-Miami equipment manager Marty Daly charged. The magazine alleged that players escaped detection by using hard-to-detect steroids as late as six weeks before the 1987 Fiesta Bowl.[9]

Another example of alleged steroid use by a team was revealed by lineman Tommy Chaikin to

Sports Illustrated in 1988. He admitted that when he played for the University of South Carolina steroid use had made him so irrational he had seriously considered shooting himself. He had a loaded .357 Magnum pointed at his chin when his father showed up outside his room and took him to a psychiatrist for help.[10]

Chaikin decided to bulk up on steroids and human growth hormones during the spring of his freshman year of college. He felt that he was too small and weak to compete with fellow USC athletes, whom he contended had been taking performance-enhancing drugs. He became, he alleges, one of thirty other users on the squad. In eight weeks, he gained twenty-five pounds and dramatically boosted his ability to lift weights. He ignored certain undesirable side effects, including shriveled testicles, high blood pressure, a heart murmur, bad acne, and hair loss. He needed only two hours of sleep daily, and the testosterone had him feeling "charged up" all the time.[11]

But he continued taking the drug after his body had become massive, because he had become a starting player for the USC Gamecocks and was afraid of losing the job if he dropped any of the drug-assisted weight. His coaches praised the new Tommy Chaikin. He began getting into fights, the rage building quickly whenever he felt confronted. After 1986, drug testing was initiated, but he substituted someone else's urine. When he got into a bar fight and was stabbed with a hunting knife, head coach Joe Morrison helped him hide the story from the press. Eventually, he alleged, half the USC team was on steroids with him.[12]

The South Carolina staff allegedly turned a blind eye to what was happening. "We threw the used syringes into the waste cans in our rooms," said

Chaikin. "We even had syringes sticking in the walls."[13]

As his play improved, his tendency toward violence became more marked. One day he threatened a pizza delivery boy with a loaded shotgun. Eventually, his liver became adversely affected, and he developed tumors that had to be surgically removed. He also began having anxiety attacks. That's when his father took him to the psychiatrist. Off steroids now, he said he continues to have physical problems, including headaches and faulty balance. "Steroids screwed me up pretty good," he admits.[14]

Professional wrestling, a sport with many detractors because of its carnival atmosphere, has had its image additionally tarnished. Evidence that some wrestlers used steroids to build more massive bodies emerged during the 1991 trial of a Pennsylvania doctor found guilty of illegally selling steroids in violation of a federal Anti–Drug Abuse Act.

The physician's records showed that he had illegally prescribed steroids for the world's best-known wrestler, Hulk Hogan, a former World Wrestling Federation (WWF) champion. Other wrestlers also purchased steroids from the doctor. Hulk Hogan and the other wrestlers escaped prosecution because they had obtained the steroids from the doctor when it was no crime to use them. (Possession and use now violate federal law. Anyone convicted can receive a jail term of up to one year and a fine of up to $100,000.)

Although Hogan and the other professional wrestlers escaped a prison sentence, they had clearly violated WWF rules forbidding use of performance-enhancing drugs.[15] Badly embarrassed by additional press reports that up to 50 percent of its athletes had purchased steroids to build massive bodies, the WWF in March 1992 announced a

$1 million program to detect usage. In addition, the WWF promised to punish wrestlers caught breaking the rules. A third offense now means automatic expulsion from the WWF.[16]

Track-and-field events have been particularly vulnerable to athletes willing to risk their future health for immediate gains in speed and strength. Without question, a steroids scandal was the biggest story of the Seoul Olympic Games in 1988.

No runner looked as fine as Ben Johnson did in winning the 100-meter event. His Greek-god muscles threatened to explode through the surface of his skin, and he had time enough at the finish to turn and mock his old foe, Carl Lewis, who finished a distant second. Despite losing a step to taunt Lewis, Johnson's time was 9.79 seconds, a world record.

A drug test, however, was positive for steroid use. After initial denials, Johnson admitted that he had used steroids from 1981 to 1988. Aided by chemicals, he set four records in the hundred-meter event, breaking the ten-second barrier four times.[17]

Because of Johnson's failed drug test, he lost his medal, his pride, and the adulation of millions of his fellow Canadian citizens. He also lost the chance to win some $10 million in endorsement contracts. Nonetheless, he later said that he had gained something far more important when his steroid use was exposed.

"Whatever I lost doesn't mean a thing," said Johnson after his suspension had ended and he had returned to racing. "My health is the most important thing. I want to have children, get married. If I had kept taking (steroids), I could have side effects with my liver. I'm very glad I got caught."[18]

Upon returning to track after his suspension, Johnson without steroids was not as successful an athlete as he had been with them. Had he not

In one of the most publicized sports scandals of all time, runner Ben Johnson of Canada was stripped of a gold medal in the 100-meter race at the Seoul, South Korea, 1988 Summer Olympics. Immediately after the race, Johnson tested positive for steroids.

cheated, it is doubtful that he could have achieved such spectacular results. Like other athletes who try to compete after stopping steroid use, Johnson's size and speed had shrunk noticeably. He finished seventh in his first race after the suspension was lifted.[19]

"He's a decent sprinter," said Tom Tellez, Ben Johnson's coach. "But he doesn't know what to do with a nonsuper body. It must be like you were once a stud horse and now you're a gelding."[20]

Ben Johnson, even without steroids, found himself involved in yet another scandal. In October 1991, the sprinter pleaded guilty to assault. He admitted assaulting former teammate Cheryl Thibedeau because he resented comments she had made about his use of steroids. Johnson received probation for the attack.[21]

Ben Johnson's comeback ended abruptly in 1993. After he tested positive for steroids a second time, the International Amateur Athletic Federation banned him for life. Unless Johnson can successfully appeal the verdict, his track career is over.

While Johnson suffered the most notoriety for his use of steroids, he was not the only top-name athlete to use them. Prior to the 1984 Olympics, eighty-six athletes failed similar drug tests. Many athletes who cheated, however, were never caught. Approximately twenty athletes who had tested clean had nonetheless used steroids, admitted Dr. Robert Kerr, the Los Angeles–based physician who had supplied them.

In addition, seven U.S. cyclists resorted to blood doping (the practice of removing a pint of blood from an athlete, pumping it full of oxygen, and replacing it just before an event) to gain an edge.[22]

The practice of blood doping can result in "a 25 percent increase in endurance" according to Swedish researchers. Among others, Dr. Bjorn Ekblom of Stockholm's Institute of Gymnastics and Sport has condemned its use to improve performance as "unethical." The seven U.S. athletes involved in the scandal included gold and silver medalist Steve Hegg, and silver medalists Rebecca Twigg, Pat McDonough, and Leonard Nitz. Nitz also won a bronze medal.[23]

Also worth noting is that the difficulty in proving precisely which athletes cheat with steroids breeds scandal itself. During the 1992 Olympics, sprinter Gwen Torrance of the United States found herself the unwanted center of attention when she finished fourth in the women's 100-meter finals and accused three of her opponents of taking steroids.

While steroid scandals prior to 1990 mainly involved professional and top amateur sports, evidence shows that scandals will now erupt on the high school level as many young athletes try to emulate athletes who have used performance-enhancing drugs. A 1992 survey conducted by the Illinois Department of Alcoholism and Substance Abuse presented some disturbing findings. Twenty-one percent of high school athletes admitting steroid use said that their supplier was a coach or teacher.[24]

One high school athlete may have paid too heavy a price for building his physique with chemicals. In 1989, *Sports Illustrated* reported the death of a heavy steroids user, Benji Ramirez, of Ashtabula (Ohio) High School. Three nights after playing a top-notch game at his defensive tackle position, Ramirez, who had a letter of interest from the Youngstown State football coach, died of an apparent heart attack. Ashtabula County coroner Dr. Robert A. Malinowski offered his opinion that steroid use contributed to the player's death.[25]

Steroid use remains a problem in sports. There

was, however, one encouraging development in 1991. The NCAA announced that only 1.1 percent of college football players tested positive for steroids, compared to a similar survey in 1989, which found that 10 percent used them. Countering that claim, several experts maintained that the 1.1 percent figure was too low, because it did not include those athletes who had learned to mask their drug use during testing. Texas A & M strength coach Mike Clark, for example, estimated that 3 to 5 percent of all players still used the performance-enhancing drugs.[26]

Clearly, until technology for testing matches the desire and wherewithal of athletes to beat the system with drugs, stories of top athletes using steroids will continue to make the news.

"So many kids . . . read the headlines, and they say, 'Well, I should try that, too. It may be dangerous, but let me give it a shot,' " Arnold Schwarzenegger told *U.S. News & World Report*. "So many kids have this misconception that all you need to do is take a few pills and work out a little bit and that will take you over the top. But that's not the way it works. That extra twenty pounds [9 kg] that you may lift from using those steroids is not going to be worth it.

"No one will know about it. But you will know when you get sick and when the side effects come out. It doesn't pay off. I think it is very important that someone like myself who has been there—someone they idolize—gets that message out."

4

ALCOHOL AND DRUG ABUSE

In June 1986, in the space of eight days, two of America's finest young athletes died from overdoses of cocaine.

One was Len Bias, a star basketball player from the University of Maryland who was drafted the Number One pick by the Boston Celtics. Bias had been touted as the player most likely to become the team's star following Larry Bird's eventual retirement. Instead, his ill-advised use of cocaine resulted in a fatal heart attack. "On a day the children mourn, I hope they learn," prayed Reverend Jesse Jackson.

The lesson was short-lived. Cleveland Browns defensive back Don Rogers died the following week while snorting cocaine in celebration of his upcoming wedding.

In recent years, drug abuse stories have become commonplace on the nation's sports pages. Bias's mother, Louise, has said that the deaths of athletes like her son are significant because they reflect what is happening to society as a whole. "Every family in this nation has been touched by substance abuse or violence," she said.[1]

The 1986 funeral of Len Bias, star University of Maryland basketball player and number one draft pick of the Boston Celtics. Bias died of a cardiac arrest related to cocaine use.

Perhaps because young people believe they are invincible, it is difficult for educators to convince them that drugs and alcohol can kill. If anyone should have been forewarned, it was the brother of Don Rogers, the Detroit Lions' first-round draft pick Reggie Rogers. But on October 20, 1988, Reggie Rogers became intoxicated and crashed his Jeep into a car of teenagers. Rogers killed three people in the accident and broke two vertebrae in his neck. Had he not been a six-six (2-m), 266-pound (121-kg) athlete blessed with above-average strength, his own life might have ended in that wreck. In 1992, after being cut by several teams, he found himself struggling to play even a reserve role in the NFL.[2]

Many all-star players have seen their careers ended or shortened by drug and/or alcohol abuse. A case in point was the career of Dexter Manley, who violated NFL substance-abuse policies four times. A veteran of two Super Bowls with Washington, Manley retired from the NFL in December 1991 and elected to play pro football in Canada rather than let the NFL suspend him again for drug use. "I know I let a lot of people down, but the biggest person I let down was Dexter," he admitted to a reporter. "You hear the old slogan, 'One day at a time,' but for me . . . it's just one minute at a time."

In one way, however, he was lucky. He still retained his life and the support of a loving family. Others have been less fortunate. In 1983, linebacker Larry Gordon of the Miami Dolphins suffered a fatal heart attack that a friend of his said was caused by free-basing cocaine.

Another athlete who came to a drug-related end was Eugene "Big Daddy" Lipscomb, a popular pro football player of the 1950s and early 1960s. At six-six (2 m) and 285 (130 kg) pounds, fast and powerful, Big Daddy was one of the most intimidating pass

Washington Redskins defensive end Dexter Manley retired from the NFL after being found in violation of NFL substance abuse policies for the fourth time.

rushers ever to play the game. Unlike most pro players, he did not go to college. He got his education in the streets of Detroit and in the U.S. Marines.[3]

But Lipscomb, who gained his greatest fame playing for the championship teams of the then Baltimore Colts, abused his body with alcohol and drugs. He could consume a fifth of whiskey as easily as another person could down a single drink. He started most days off with a dozen eggs, a pound of bacon, and a pint of alcohol. Feeling invincible, he never felt he had to curtail his drinking.[4]

At some point in his thirties, Lipscomb abused heroin as well as alcohol. On May 10, 1963, he died of a combination of the two substances. His alcohol-damaged liver, an autopsy showed, failed to remove the heroin and alcohol from his system. The cause of death was acute alcohol poisoning.[5]

Another heavy price to pay for drug use was paid by former professional baseball star Alan Wiggins, a longtime drug user who died at thirty-two in 1991. His cause of death was complications caused by AIDS, possibly acquired by sharing needles with a drug abuser who had the virus.

Blessed with above-average skills, in 1980 Wiggins excited the San Diego Padres management when he stole 120 bases in their minor league system. He was called up to the majors in 1981, but in 1982 drew a suspension from the baseball commissioner's office because he had been caught using cocaine.[6]

Given another chance in 1983, Wiggins hit .276 for the Padres. His speed electrified crowds, and he tied the major-league record for most stolen bases in a single game with five. He stole seventy bases in 1984 (a team record), and played in a World Series for San Diego, hitting .364. In 1985, after the Padres offered him a $2.5 million multiyear contract, he suffered another drug relapse and was traded to Baltimore. Before the season was over, he had again used drugs and was banned from baseball by the commissioner's office. His career was over, and he never overcame his addiction to drugs. He weighed only seventy pounds when he died.[7]

Many baseball players destroyed or came close to destroying their careers by using cocaine. One of the most widely publicized scandals in Major League Baseball history was a 1985 drug trial in Pittsburgh that implicated no less than twenty-one players (many of them present or former Pirates) as drug users. Until that trial, baseball administrators had steadfastly denied that players had drug problems. Drug use "has never come up, and I don't think it ever will," National League president Warren Giles told *Sports Illustrated* in 1969.

During the 1980s, several players accumulated arrest records for drug possession. Onetime Cy Young Award–winning pitcher LaMarr Hoyt of San Diego was arrested four times on charges of possession and/or distribution of marijuana, cocaine, Valium, and Quaaludes. The Padres released him, ending his career, and a federal judge sentenced him to one year in prison.[8]

Hoyt had long had a reputation for getting into trouble off the field, incurring four arrests on various charges, so his downfall came as no surprise to baseball fans. But most fans expressed shock when clean-cut Dwight Gooden, the star pitcher of the New York Mets, checked into Smithers Alcoholism and Drug Treatment Center in 1987. The Mets had survived scandal the previous year when first baseman Keith Hernandez admitted he had used cocaine. Baseball commissioner Peter Ueberroth suspended Hernandez and six other players for their involvement with drugs. The suspensions were later lifted when the players agreed to certain conditions, such as random drug testing and community service. Also implicated in the scandal were baseball players Lee Lacy, Al Holland, Claudell Washington, and Larry Sorenson.[9]

Many players even used controlled substances on the field. Former Pittsburgh pitcher Dock Ellis actually once pitched a game on LSD. Even more surprising, he allowed no hits in that 1970 win. Ellis's career was shortened by his addiction to drugs and alcohol, but he later overcame his problem and became a counselor.[10]

Drug problems continue today. In March 1992, New York Yankee pitcher Pascual Perez failed to show up for spring training. He had tested positive for drugs. His teammate, pitcher Steve Howe, was banned from baseball for drug use the same year, although he later managed to convince major league baseball to allow him yet another chance to play.

Howe's suspension came after he had repeatedly tried to overcome his problem. The commissioner's office gave the 1980 Major League rookie of the year seven chances. The 1992 ban occurred after Howe admitted in a drug trial that he had purchased cocaine the previous off-season in his Whitefish, Montana, hometown.

Like Dock Ellis, Howe said he had used drugs during baseball games, snorting cocaine in the bull pen when he was used as a relief pitcher. The drug also hurt his family. He disappeared on a cocaine binge while his wife was in the hospital with their newborn child. And the cost of buying drugs, in part, made this player—who had earned millions of dollars—file for bankruptcy.

Some players have turned their lives around after a suspension. In 1991, Atlanta Braves outfielder Otis Nixon deprived himself of a chance for

Star relief pitcher Steve Howe (left) of the New York Yankees pleaded guilty to a federal drug misdemeanor charge in Missoula, Montana, in 1992. Howe has been suspended from the game seven times for violating professional baseball's strictures against alcohol and drug abuse.

glory and let his team down when the commissioner's office refused to let him play in the World Series because he had failed a drug test. Nixon, who had previously received treatment for a drug problem in 1987, called his suspension a blessing in disguise. He told the press that the suspension was what it took to wake him up. "The toughest thing was admitting that I was whipped by a problem, by a disease," he told the press.

Drug problems are not peculiar to professional baseball. College and NBA basketball have also had their drug scandals.

In 1987, Gary McLain, star of the 1985 national championship Villanova basketball team, admitted that he had played while under the influence of cocaine in many games, including the semifinal victory over Memphis State during the NCAA Final Four. He was also on drugs, he said, when President Ronald Reagan greeted him and his teammates at the White House.[11]

Seven players have been banned for life from the NBA for similar drug problems. In October 1991, basketball star Roy Tarpley of the Dallas Mavericks became the last NBA player to lose his livelihood in that fashion after he refused to take a mandatory drug test. Tarpley, who forfeited his $3 million salary for the '91–'92 season, had two previous suspensions for drugs.[12]

College and professional football have also been rocked by allegations of drug use. One scandal erupted twenty-four hours before the start of the Super Bowl in 1989, when Cincinnati coaches discovered running back Stanley Wilson using cocaine in his hotel room. The career of Wilson, one of the leading rushers in the NFL, ended with that incident.

Wilson wasn't the only athlete to play under the influence of drugs in a Super Bowl. Onetime Dal-

Thomas "Hollywood" Henderson, ex–Dallas Cowboys defensive star, serving time in prison after his conviction on charges of sexual offenses against two teenage girls and subsequently attempting to bribe them to drop the charges. Henderson was also an admitted cocaine user and even snorted the drug during the Super Bowl.

las Cowboys superstar Thomas "Hollywood" Henderson, an admitted cocaine addict, in 1979 used a Vicks inhaler to put a gram and a half of cocaine into his nose prior to the start of Super Bowl XIII against Pittsburgh. He played the whole game with the Vicks inhaler in his pocket, taking it out on the sidelines to snort cocaine during the televised game.[13]

Like many athletes who use drugs, Henderson rationalized the need for drugs because of the physical pain caused by chronic sports injuries. Cartilage tears, wrenched knees, arthritic joints, and slipped vertebrae are commonly suffered by athletes. Because players might not play as effectively when in pain, many professional clubs indiscriminately gave out pain pills. While injured players can get through a game, a season, maybe even a career on pain relievers, some become addicted. Others proceed to unlawful street drugs, telling themselves that these drugs, too, are needed to medicate pain.

Hollywood Henderson notes that he didn't step onto a professional football field one day and snort cocaine because he felt like it. For many years, he took prescription drugs to get his body through game after game. "The drugs that I abused playing the game, and that were abused by almost everybody around me, were codeine, Percodan, and amphetamines," Henderson has admitted. "Codeine kills pain. Percodan kills pain."[14]

Henderson, an illegitimate son born to a fifteen-year-old mother, grew up in Austin, Texas. He spent his boyhood watching his mother and stepfather drink and argue while under the influence of alcohol. Like many alcohol and drug abusers, he had poor role models.[15]

Many other football stars have found themselves in legal trouble because of drug problems.

Linebacker Lawrence Taylor was suspended twice for drug abuse by the NFL during his career with the New York Giants.[16] Todd Marinovich, the quarterback for the Oakland Raiders, finished his college career at Southern California with a misdemeanor arrest for cocaine possession. In 1992, former New York Giants defensive back Larry Flowers admitted that he'd played under the influence of cocaine from 1980 to 1986.[17]

Drug scandals have involved stars of many other major sports, and the problems extend outside the borders of the United States. Several international players have admitted drug use. When Argentina's national soccer team captain, Diego Maradona, was arrested for possession of cocaine his drug problem became headline news in virtually every country of the world.[18]

Few major sports have escaped drug scandals. Professional hockey star Grant Fuhr admitted in 1991 that he had been taking cocaine for seven years. His professional career could have been over had the NHL chosen to ban him. Instead, then National Hockey League president John Ziegler accepted Fuhr's word that he had conquered the drug problem.[19] Not so fortunate was Bob Probert, a Detroit hockey player caught trying to smuggle cocaine from Canada into the United States. He received a three-month jail sentence and was suspended by the NHL for what amounted to one year. In addition, he returned on only a part-time basis because the U.S. Immigration Bureau refused to allow him to play in Canada.[20]

Another hockey player whose excessive use of alcohol, steroids, and cocaine brought him trouble was John Kordic, a brawling, bad-tempered player for a series of NHL clubs, including the 1985 Stanley Cup–winning Montreal Canadiens and the Quebec

Substance abuse caused the untimely death of hockey star John Kordic, shown here (at left) celebrating a goal scored while a player with the Montreal Canadiens.

Nordiques. In and out of substance abuse clinics, Kordic was never able to defeat his addictions, and he was relegated to playing for an Edmonton minor league team. His behavior both on the ice and off became erratic, and he was once arrested for physically threatening his girlfriend.

Friends warned him that his substance abuse would lead to his death, but he couldn't or wouldn't reform. In the summer of 1992, he obtained a supply of steroids and checked into a seedy motel near Quebec City, where he began to rage out of control, frightening employees. Police handcuffed him and put him in an ambulance, but he never made it to a hospital. The twenty-seven-year-old Kordic died handcuffed and bound to a stretcher. At the time of his death, the Edmonton Oilers were contemplating signing him to a contract that would have enabled him to make a comeback.[21]

Many professional racers have been arrested for illegal drug use. In March 1992, drag racer Darrell Alderman, a two-time National Hot Rod Association champion, received a light sentence despite charges of intending to distribute cocaine. By cooperating with authorities, Alderman was given five years' probation. He could have been sentenced to five years in a federal prison.

Like drugs, alcohol has ruined the lives of many athletes. Jockey Bill Shoemaker, Olympic diver Bruce Kimball, and hockey player Pelle Lindbergh have had automobile accidents with tragic consequences. Baseball players Mark Portugal, Don Newcombe, and Sam McDowell, hampered by their addiction to alcohol, performed at less than their best in ball games.

In May 1991, two members of the Philadelphia Phillies left a bachelor party for teammate John Kruk. The driver, Lenny Dykstra, had been drinking. He lost control of his Mercedes, smashing into two trees and severely injuring his passenger, catcher Darren Daulton. Dykstra's blood-alcohol level was .18, the equivalent of drinking eight beers in one hour, making him legally drunk by Pennsylvania law. He suffered multiple injuries—a broken right cheekbone, a punctured lung, a broken collarbone, and three broken ribs.[22]

Many people in baseball chided Dykstra for putting the lives of innocent people, as well as his passenger and himself, in jeopardy. Few people who knew Dykstra well were surprised by his accident, wrote columnist Bob Nightengale in the *Sporting News*. "No one feels sorry for you," wrote Nightengale. "The only thing you've managed to save is your life, and you almost blew that, too."[23]

Dykstra not only lived but managed to play baseball again. Billy Martin, the fiery ex-manager of the New York Yankees, was not as fortunate. He died in an alcohol-related accident on Christmas Day, 1989, after he and a friend had been drinking in a Binghamton, New York, bar. Police charged Martin's friend with driving while intoxicated.

As a player, alcohol had often gotten the best of Martin. His career as a New York Yankee second baseman ended after a brawl at the Copacabana nightclub. In spite of his talent, the team traded him. The fight was a national scandal, involving star Yankees Mickey Mantle, Yogi Berra, Johnny Kucks, and Hank Bauer, as well as Martin.

As a manager of the Yankees, Martin's drinking involved him in several scrapes that made sports headlines. Following the 1979 season, Martin punched out a marshmallow salesman in a bar with a single blow. The Yankees promptly fired him. Rehired in 1983, Martin got into another argument in a California bar. The club fired him again. In 1985,

Former New York Yankees manager Billy Martin looks to be still smarting a few days after a 1988 barroom altercation. Martin died tragically in an alcohol-related car accident in 1989.

the Yankees again took a chance on him, but Martin shoved a fan in a Baltimore bar, and again lost his job. Hoping he had learned a lesson, the Yankees rehired Martin in 1988, only to fire him halfway through the season after he was injured in a brawl in a Texas bar.[24]

Playing baseball has also put other baseball stars under such pressure that they've sought to escape their problems by drinking. When outfielder Darryl Strawberry played for the Mets, he began to drink heavily. He failed to show up for a game one day, claiming he had had a flat tire. Another day, during a photo session, he picked a fight with teammate Keith Hernandez. Strawberry also took his problems home, and he nearly lost his marriage. Realizing that he and his career were both in trouble, in 1990 he checked into an alcoholism and treatment center.[25]

Strawberry, to his credit, managed to curb his addiction to alcohol. But like all alcoholics, he knows that he must live one day at a time and can never take the risk of consuming a single drink. "I don't even miss it," said Strawberry, four months after leaving an alcohol rehabilitation center. "I'm very happy with my life, so there's no reason to ever take a drink again."[26]

Even in the early days of professional baseball, alcohol problems plagued athletes. During the nineteenth century, King Kelly—the most exciting, best-paid player of his day—drank himself to death at the age of thirty-six. Other well-known alcoholic stars of baseball's infant era included pitchers Terry Larkin and Rube Waddell, outfielder Chief Sockalexis, and pitcher-outfielder James Egan. They died unnaturally young deaths because of alcohol abuse.

Like Darryl Strawberry, pitcher Dennis Eckersley was one of the fortunate ones who was able to defeat his addiction. He began drinking at age twenty, when he first made it into the major leagues. He says he was soon drinking both to celebrate and to forget his problems, becoming a full-fledged alcoholic. In 1980, his drinking resulted in the end of his first marriage. Eckersley subsequently married Nancy O'Neil, who disapproved of her husband's drinking. It took six years, and the near disintegration of his career, before he sought treatment prior to the 1987 season.

The results were dramatic. After graduating from a rehabilitation center, Eckersley became the premier relief pitcher in baseball. He stayed sober while starring for the Oakland Athletics, and his record as a reliever makes him a good candidate for election to Baseball's Hall of Fame. "People don't realize what alcohol can do to a person," he once said. "It jeopardized my career and my relationship with my wife, which is more important to me."

Other players have also beaten alcohol, including Eckersley's teammate, pitcher Bob Welch. Like Eckersley, Welch squandered his talent for many years until he realized that he had to face his problems. "Sobriety is something I must deal with every day," says the ace of the Athletics' staff. His drinking began in bars while attending high school in suburban Detroit, escalated in college at Eastern Michigan University, and jeopardized his major league career when he showed up drunk at a game. He had to be led away after trying to pick a fight with an opposing player.[27]

That scandal, along with too many embarrassing morning-afters, woke him up. In 1980, he attended an Arizona rehab center and saved his career and probably his life as well. He continues to attend Alcoholics Anonymous meetings.

Bowler Pete Weber also turned his life around after finding himself in double jeopardy, addicted to both alcohol and cocaine since high school. The son of another bowling legend, Dick Weber, Pete endured what his father called "eight years of hell" until he checked himself into a Missouri rehabilitation center. In two years, Pete had spent $150,000 on drugs and alcohol.

"From the first line of coke I ever did, I was hooked," Pete Weber once said, admitting that he had also gotten himself up to a fifth of Jack Daniel's a night. His addiction reached a point at which he could no longer bowl without using cocaine. He suffered blackouts, unable to even remember the games he bowled. His addiction affected his family life, and for a time his wife and daughter left him. He even lost many fans, who no longer tolerated his tantrums during bowling matches.[28]

Weber finally sought professional help. By entering a treatment center he was able to turn his life around. During his first sober tournament, the young bowler announced where he'd been and said that he no longer would be going out for drinks after bowling. His fellow pros cheered him.

Another success story concerns the recovery from alcoholism of Chris Mullin, star of the NBA Golden State Warriors, whose offense and defense on the court had suffered from his addiction. After Mullin obtained counseling and stopped drinking, he became one of the NBA's star players and was named to the 1992 U.S. Olympic team.

One of the most stirring stories about players who have beaten an addiction to cocaine was John Lucas. He failed to recover until he had been suspended by the NBA for drug use three times. "As an athlete I'd always been taught to try to win at any cost, but in order to beat this disease I finally realized I had to surrender to it," Lucas told *Sports Illustrated*.

Lucas, like Hollywood Henderson, has become an anti–substance abuse crusade. Both have tremendous influence with players because they are living examples of how talent can be squandered. "There *is* life after drugs," Henderson wrote in his autobiography. "Just don't die trying to find that life. Don't take that first drink of alcohol or use drugs. Please!"[29]

Lucas went beyond saving his own life, and after successfully coaching a semiprofessional team made up exclusively of former NBA players who were recovering substance abusers, returned to the NBA as a coach.

5

RACISM

America's longest continuous sports scandal was Major League Baseball's refusal for more than half a century to allow blacks to play baseball. A collusion of owners excluded blacks for no reason other than the racial prejudice of white America.

The color line in baseball was drawn in 1887, the year manager Cap Anson of Chicago's National League team waged a campaign to keep the New York Giants from signing a talented black ballplayer named George Stovey. Anson's private war escalated in 1888, when he successfully lobbied against attempts by several major league owners to sign talented black players. As a result, major leaguer brothers Welday and Moses Fleetwood Walker were banned from the game, along with some twenty-five others who had been in the minor leagues. "After Cap Anson drew the color line," said Daniel Okrent and Harris Lewine, editors of *The Ultimate Baseball Book,* "Welday wrote the President of the Tri-State League, George McDermott: 'The rule that you have passed is a public disgrace.' "

So it was. And the public disgrace would exist

Manager Adrian (Cap) Anson lobbied vigorously to keep blacks out of baseball in the 1880s. The "color line" remained for another sixty years.

in professional baseball for fifty-odd years, depriving fans of the privilege of watching black players such as catcher Josh Gibson, who was said to be every bit as good a batter as Babe Ruth. The color barrier wasn't broken until April 18, 1946, when Jackie Robinson played for Montreal of the International League against Jersey City. In his second at bat, Robinson hit a home run, one of his four hits in that game, figuratively shattering the color barrier with one mighty swing.[1]

Robinson was signed by Branch Rickey of the Brooklyn Dodgers. Robinson might have entered professional ball one year earlier, when in 1945 he and another black player, Sam Jethroe, tried out for the Boston Red Sox. But an angry Red Sox administrator told some of his employees to escort the blacks from the field, denying them the opportunity to try out.[2]

Robinson and Jethroe lost their opportunity to play because the management of the Red Sox feared that white fans in Boston might stop coming to games. And according to many black professional sports stars who have encountered problems there, prejudice in Boston against black players continues to this day.[3]

Boston's legacy of hate has drawn comment from both journalists and black players. The Red Sox were the last big-league baseball club to sign a black player. And since the U.S. Supreme Court mandated forced busing of students in the 1970s, some say the hatred of whites toward blacks has escalated. Forced busing in Boston led to many angry confrontations between the races.

So even though integration is an accepted fact on most big-league baseball clubs today, the Red Sox have been an unpleasant exception. Racism in Boston is "almost an impossible thing to shake," Red

Jackie Robinson was the first black player in the major leagues. He is shown here at his 1949 contract signing with Brooklyn Dodgers president Branch Rickey (right). That season, his third in the majors, he would win the National League Most Valuable Player award.

Sox president John Harrington admitted to the press. Consequently, opportunities for black players with Boston were no better in 1991 than they were in the early 1950s. In 1991, the Red Sox began the year with a single black player on the roster.[4]

Black athletes in many sports have reported racial bias in Boston. Former Celtic M. L. Carr charges that his wife was verbally assaulted while standing with the couple's children on a street curb. Another Celtic, Dee Brown, was forced to the ground at gunpoint in a Boston suburb by police who thought that he resembled a black bank robber.[5]

But Jackie Robinson's problems were not limited to visits to Boston while playing the National League Braves (now in Atlanta). In some cities he was denied access to the same restaurants and hotels his teammates patronized. He had to eat on buses or sleep in inferior motels, not only in the South, but also in cities as far north as Philadelphia.

To try to distract him from his game, rival players taunted and verbally abused him. The manager of the Philadelphia Phillies, Ben Chapman, was an Alabama native who was not shy about expressing his disdain for Jews and Negroes. He and his teams made vicious and obscene remarks about Robinson when the black ballplayer played against the Phillies. Chapman's tirades were mean and stereotypical, forcing then-commissioner of baseball Happy Chandler to step in and stop the abuse. Robinson had been ordered by Rickey not to fight back, because he would only hurt the chances of other blacks to make the majors.[6]

Robinson had little respite off the field, drawing bags full of hate mail. Many letters contained threats of death to him or harm to his family. The Phillies heard about the death threats and during games made machine-gun noises to rattle him. He also became a favorite target of pitchers who tried to intimidate him by aiming for his head.[7]

Nonetheless, Robinson's trials led to many improvements in race relations in American society as a whole as in sports. His breaking of the so-called color barrier in baseball was a major milestone in the struggle to give blacks equal employment opportunities. While it is true that many black players suffered by never getting a shot at playing in the majors, they were not the only losers. Baseball fans and the game itself were cheated from seeing many potential Hall of Famers. Apologizing to black players at a Negro Leagues reunion in Cooperstown in 1991, then-Commissioner Fay Vincent noted that "Baseball was deprived . . . because it didn't have Josh (Gibson), it didn't have Cool Papa (Bell), and it didn't have Satchel (Paige), at least not in his prime."[8]

Robinson was not the only black ballplayer to suffer insults and attacks. As a boy, Henry Aaron sat in the colored section of Hartwell Field in his native Mobile, Alabama, and although Robinson had broken the color barrier, by 1953 only six major-league teams had signed blacks. Consequently, Aaron had to be discovered while playing for the Indianapolis Clowns of the Negro Leagues.

Throughout his memorable career as a player, Aaron faced torrents of abuse from white bigots. In 1973, while trying to tie and break Babe Ruth's career home run mark of 714, he endured racist treatment similar to what Jackie Robinson had suffered. Even fans in Atlanta, his home ballpark, taunted him about his skin color. The fact that a black man had a chance to set the all-time home-run record was resented by some whites. A few racists might even have killed him to protect Ruth's record. Death threats against Hank Aaron became so numerous

Henry Aaron, the all-time home run king of major league baseball, endured racial bigotry throughout his career.

that the FBI had to investigate. What particularly frightened him were threats made against his family. Someone even contemplated kidnapping his daughter, who was away at college.[9]

In his autobiography, *I Had a Hammer,* Aaron revealed the specifics of these threats. Many contained the most vile language imaginable. In the same book, the slugger reported that he was relieved as well as happy when he hit home runs 714 and 715, putting the Babe—and racists in America—largely behind him when the record fell.[10]

Aaron's heroics made it easier for young blacks to get an opportunity to play ball, because one time, even black athletes competing in amateur sports had to endure abuse. In an emotional essay for *Sports Illustrated,* former Oakland slugger Reggie Jackson talked about the hurt he felt as a young teenager playing baseball. Jackson, the son of a ballplayer who had toiled in the Negro Leagues, had been elected to an all-star team from his native Pennsylvania, but he was humiliated by being allowed only a single at bat because his coach and the rival team from Florida feared a racial incident.

"I lived two miles from the park, and I walked home, crying," admitted Jackson. "Every step of the way, I said to myself 'I'm going to be a big leaguer,' I'm going to be a big leaguer.' "[11]

Things didn't get much easier for Jackson while playing in the minor leagues. After being hit in the head with a pitch in Lewiston, Idaho, a hospital there refused to admit him because he was black. Later, playing for Birmingham, Alabama, a white landlord threatened to evict him and two white roommates because he was black. Jackson had to move to a hotel. Because many restaurants in the South refused to serve black players, the whole team ate many of its meals on the team bus in a display of unity.[12]

Although today opportunities for blacks are better, baseball has not totally erased its racial bias. Blacks in baseball continue to fight racism, charging that minorities are too often overlooked when there are management openings. Baseball failed to hire a black manager until Frank Robinson found a job piloting the Cleveland Indians in 1975. In 1992, there were only two minority managers of major league teams, Hal McRae with Kansas City and Cito Gaston with Toronto, until Montreal hired Felipé Alou, a native of the Dominican Republic, in midseason. Whites filled thirteen of fourteen vacancies for big-league managers in 1991. Also in 1991, not one manager at Triple A, the highest level of baseball's minor leagues, was black.

Richard Lapchick, director of a Northeastern University–based organization, the Center for the Study of Sport in Society, charged that major league baseball lags woefully behind pro football and basketball when it comes to hiring minorities. "It is very disheartening to see how little progress has been made in major league baseball," said Lapchick. To cite an example, Lapchick noted that not one black was working as a baseball general manager.[13]

According to Hank Aaron, now senior vice president of the Atlanta Braves, blacks are kept out of baseball management because of an old-boy network at the general-manager level. He cites two black players who have been deprived of opportunities to manage. "You look at a guy like Ernie Banks and what he meant to the Chicago Cubs," says Aaron, referring to Banks's Hall of Fame credentials as a shortstop. "He's out of baseball. Billy Williams [another famous ex-Chicago player] can't even find a job. . . . I don't know if it's a conspiracy or just what it is."[14]

One black managerial candidate who had been passed over several times expressed frustration at his inability to find a position. Don Baylor, a player for seventeen years and batting coach for two, said in 1991 that he was tired of being told he wasn't managerial material because "players are in awe of you." Argued Baylor, "It makes you wonder, what are they [general managers] afraid of."[15]

Baylor won his fight in 1993, becoming the manager of the Colorado Rockies in the National League. The National League's San Francisco Giants also hired a black manager, Dusty Baker, for the 1993 season.

Perhaps some are not afraid, but may be ignorant, letting prejudice get in the way of their judgment. This was true when Los Angeles Dodgers vice president Al Campanis defended baseball's poor record in hiring blacks, saying that they might lack the "necessities" for achieving success in sports management. Speaking on the nationally televised *Nightline* in April of 1987, Campanis destroyed his career as he made one racist comment after another.

Campanis denied that prejudice was to blame for the lack of blacks in baseball executive positions, saying "they may not have the desire to be in the front office."

Such thinking extends even to the front offices of college athletic departments. In 1991, less than 2 percent of the 68,000 jobs in college athletic departments belonged to blacks.[16]

The Dodgers fired Campanis for the remark, ending his more than forty years in baseball. Many blacks who had been overlooked for jobs insisted that Campanis was only saying what many other white executives believed.[17] As a result, even though baseball began interviewing a few more black managers whenever a vacancy opened, it has not become a model of diversity.

Campanis was not the only person to expose his

racial biases on national television. Jimmy "the Greek" Snyder was hired by CBS Sports to appeal to fans who wanted sports news they could use for gambling. But Snyder apparently believed that his knowledge of gambling also made him an expert on the subject of race. As a result, he wound up giving an interview to an NBC affiliate on blacks in sports. The interview deservedly cost him his job.

Snyder made comments rife with stereotypes about blacks, and he attacked the notion that blacks deserved more coaching jobs. "Well, they've got everything," he told interviewer Ed Hoatling. "If they take over coaching like everybody wants them to, there's not going to be anything left for the white people."

Snyder was out of work twenty-four hours after the incident. He has since apologized for his remarks.

In 1992, Marge Schott, the owner of the Cincinnati Reds, admitted that she had used a racial slur to describe her ballplayers, claiming that she had meant the term in a humorous context. Few, if any, blacks in baseball thought her choice of words funny. "There is no place for it in the national pastime," Atlanta vice president Henry Aaron told the *Cincinnati Enquirer*. "This is ... heavier than what brought down Al Campanis."

Baseball is not the only sport that has failed to provide opportunities for players of color. With so many black players dominating professional basketball today, it is easy to overlook the fact that the NBA didn't sign an African-American player until 1950. The New York Knicks' Joe Lapchick, the first coach to sign a black, Nat "Sweetwater" Clinton, was verbally assaulted by many racists. His son, Richard Lapchick, the aforementioned director of the Center for the Study of Sport and Society, recalls

Nat "Sweetwater" Clinton, first black player to be awarded a National Basketball Association contract, and the man who signed him, New York Knicks coach Joe Lapchick.

answering the phone many times in his youth, and being shocked to hear anonymous callers shouting insults against his father.[18]

Although black players had long been a part of college basketball, they were not taken seriously by coaches until 1966, when seven black players from the Texas Western (now called University of Texas at El Paso) Miners defeated all-white Kentucky, says *Sports Illustrated* writer Curry Kirkpatrick. The significance of the game was that Texas Western had at long last made Wildcat head coach Adolph Rupp a supporter of integrated teams, and others followed his example. Before that win, not one player in the Atlantic Coast and Southeastern Conferences had been black.[19]

At a reunion of that championship team in 1991, then, and current coach Clem Haskins told the players it was their superior play that had persuaded the Kentuckys, Dukes, and Vanderbilts to integrate. "You guys got a lot of black kids scholarships around this country," Haskins told them. "You can be proud of that. I guess you helped change the world a little bit."[20]

All the El Paso players came from large urban centers, including Houston, New York, Detroit, and Gary. Previously, many coaches had ignored ghetto players, but now they began recruiting them in large numbers. That 1966 Kentucky team was the last segregated team ever to make the NCAA finals. In 1967, black superstar Lew Alcindor (later to be known as Kareem Abdul-Jabbar) took control over center court for UCLA, and college coaches everywhere began to look for dominating players regardless of race. A similar shift to using black players also took place in the NBA.

By the late 1980s, blacks so dominated both college and pro basketball that some coaches have elected to play less-talented whites instead of blacks to please white fans. For example, when Virginia Commonwealth basketball coach Sonny Smith was at Auburn, he said he felt pressure from school boosters to play whites, according to the *Montgomery Advertiser*.[21]

In 1991, Charles Barkley accused his own team, the Philadelphia 76ers, of racism, saying that the team placated white fans by keeping one less-talented white player and cutting a better black player. Otherwise, Philadelphia would be fielding an all-black team. Even though Barkley also criticized black teammates when he felt their play was inferior, he was traded in 1992, his bluntness making him unpopular with team management.

Racism has also existed in sports at the international level, most notably in South Africa. In 1964, that country refused to send a team made up of black and white athletes to the Olympics in Tokyo. The International Olympic Committee responded by banning South Africa for its racially discriminatory policy of apartheid.[22]

South Africa did not allow black athletes to compete on its international teams until 1991, when its government voted to abolish racial segregation.[23] Subsequently, even though equality between the races has yet to be achieved in South Africa, the IOC risked criticism by allowing South Africa to participate in the 1992 Olympics in Barcelona, Spain.

The issue of the Olympics and race was also a major story during the 1968 Mexico City Games. Two determined U.S. black athletes, Tommie Smith and John Carlos, protested the treatment of blacks in the United States after the two had finished first and third respectively in the 200-meter dash. Their single act of defiance was to raise black-gloved fists in the air during the playing of the national anthem.

The two said they were trying to point out that too little progress toward equality had been accomplished in America. In 1968, Martin Luther King had been assassinated. Black Freedom Riders had been abused, threatened and beaten by mobs, and imprisoned. In the world of sports, black athletes had made only a token entry, finding no opportunities in coaching and administration, as well as limited opportunities on the field.

Immediately after their protest, Smith and Carlos were regarded as traitors by many white Americans who viewed their protest in the stands or on television. The two were suspended and sent home from the Mexico City Olympics in disgrace.[24]

It took many years for white Americans to see that the peaceful protests of Smith and Carlos had taken immense courage. These two black men were vilified by many Americans who did not want the failings of the United States pointed out to the world. Nonetheless, in the long run, the protest worked, effectively demonstrating that people of color in the United States wanted exclusionary policies ended. "They do not return in disgrace, but as the honorable young men they are, dedicated to the cause of justice for the black people in our society," said San Jose State University president Robert Clark.[25]

Prejudice has even affected high school athletes in the United States. Although a golf course rarely prohibits blacks from playing at the professional level (as happened in 1990 at the Shoal Creek Country Club in Alabama during a PGA tournament), discrimination occurs much more frequently when a club's management thinks its exclusionary policies won't be noted by the press.

In 1991, the St. Frederick Catholic High School team, scheduled to play at the Caldwell Parish Country Club in Louisiana, was told that black golfer Dondré Green would not be permitted to play on the private course. The state attorney general termed the incident a case of racial discrimination, since the team had been invited to play at the club and only Green had been disinvited. To protest the country club's action, the remaining members of the St. Frederick team refused to play, forfeiting two matches.[26]

Another high school racial dispute that made national headlines in 1989 involved Conway High School in Conway, South Carolina. The situation began out of a disagreement between a coach and a black player. The coach, Chuck Jordan, said that he had shifted a black quarterback to defensive back because he had not followed orders on the field. He maintained that the quarterback had run with the ball when he had been ordered to hand it to a running back.

The black quarterback, Carlos Hunt, left the team, taking thirty-one of its thirty-seven black players with him. He contended that the coach's decision to play a white instead of him was racially motivated. The team finished with a dismal 1–11 record because of the boycott.[27]

On one side of the dispute was Jordan, who defended himself by noting that he had started a black quarterback in three of his six seasons as coach. On the other side was a local minister, Rev. H. H. Singleton, who accused the coach of "callous . . . racial intolerance." Backing the coach was the South Carolina Human Rights Commission. Opposing him was the NAACP. The town was hopelessly split along racial lines in the dispute between the white coach and the black player. The coach received death threats. The quarterback lost an opportunity to play and possibly win a scholarship to a major school.[28]

The Conway incident ended in an unpleasant stalemate, with each side vilifying the other. One reason supporters of the black quarterback fought so hard was because some white coaches have deprived blacks of an opportunity to play positions that require the ability to think. Such actions are clearly racist because they reflect unfair racial stereotypes.

Such discrimination may start in high school, but it doesn't end there. According to *USA Today,* professional football coaches refuse to play blacks at quarterback unless the black athletes perform far better than their white counterparts. The problem is caused by a practice known as "stacking," the placement of blacks and whites in positions according to racial stereotypes.[29]

"The expectations set for a black quarterback are always a lot higher," black Houston quarterback Warren Moon told the *Washington Post.* "We have to perform at a lot higher level in order to stick around."[30]

The practice of stacking is also prevalent in college football. Those coaches who disavow the notion that blacks cannot play quarterback consider themselves realists, not racists, said former black Washington quarterback Doug Williams. When such coaches draft a fast, talented black quarterback, they tend to convert him to a defensive back, he said. "Whites don't believe they're prejudiced," he said. "They believe that's just the way it is: Blacks don't play quarterback because they just aren't good enough."[31]

Racism can come from people of all skin colors. Thus, on occasion, blacks are involved in reverse discrimination. According to sportscaster Howard Cosell, in 1989, when black center Alonzo Mourning played for Georgetown, he allegedly made racist remarks to Nadav Henefeld, a player from Israel. In an attempt to distract Henefeld's attention from the game, Mourning supposedly called Henefeld a "dirty Jew." Since Mourning's coach, John Thompson, is a

Houston Oilers' quarterback Warren Moon. Many believe that expectations for black quarterbacks are often much higher than for whites.

black man who is always outspoken on matters that reflect racism, it was revealing that he neither punished his player nor asked him to apologize.[32]

And when Darryl Strawberry, a black ballplayer, was with the New York Mets, he inflamed many people in the press by angrily denouncing his teammate, Wally Backman, as a "redneck."

In another highly publicized scandal, basketball star Dennis Rodman of the Detroit Pistons lashed out at former Boston superstar Larry Bird. "Why does he get so much publicity?" snapped Rodman, following his club's defeat to the Celtics in the 1988 Eastern Conference finals. "Because he's white. You never hear about a black player being the greatest." To further ignite the controversy, veteran Isiah Thomas backed the then-rookie Rodman's words, saying that if Bird were black like he, "he'd be just another good guy."

To defuse the scandal, the NBA called a damage-control press conference in which Thomas and Rodman apologized. "I shouldn't have said what I said," said Rodman. "I made a mistake."[33]

Racism isn't limited to the playing field and administrative offices of sports teams. The bias against blacks apparently extends to the sporting goods industry, charges Ron Williams, chairman of the Association of Black Sporting Goods Professionals. "The industry, for whatever reason, has locked out blacks," he says. Equal Employment Opportunity Commission statistics validate his claim. Only 2.8 percent of all sports equipment managers are black.[34]

Clearly, although professional sports have tried to eliminate racism, its nasty specter still exists. As the Los Angeles riots of 1992 demonstrated, racism continues to be a problem in the country as a whole, just as it is in sports.

6

SEX SCANDALS

The former heavyweight boxing champion's fate was in the hands of an Indianapolis jury. The charges against Mike Tyson were serious: rape and criminal deviant conduct.

During the trial, an eighteen-year-old beauty queen and college student from Rhode Island contended that on July 19, 1991, Tyson "turned mean" after inviting her to his Indianapolis hotel room at 2 A.M. Desiree Washington said that the boxer sexually attacked and raped her on the bed. The young woman testified that the boxer had lured her to his room, saying that he only wanted to talk. Because her dad was a fan of Tyson's, Washington said that she had come hoping to take his photograph.[1]

In his defense Tyson contended that he and the Miss Black America contestant had mutually agreed to have sex. He claimed that she filed her rape charge to retaliate because he lost interest in her afterward.

The jury had other testimony that gave Washington's charges more credibility. Rosie Jones, Miss Black America of 1990, testified that Tyson had im-

Mike Tyson, former heavyweight boxing champion, being escorted from court after his 1992 rape conviction.

properly touched her and made suggestive remarks at the same Miss Black America pageant Washington had entered.[2] In addition, a female limousine driver, Virginia Foster, complained that Tyson had also tried to molest her in his hotel room. At one point, said Foster under oath, the boxer had committed a lewd act in her presence.[3]

The evidence went against Tyson. The jury voted to convict. It did not believe that Washington willingly had sexual relations with the accused. The judge sentenced Tyson to a maximum of sixty years in prison. Even with time off, should he be a model prisoner, he would have to serve a minimum of three to six years.[4]

Once in prison, Tyson was the opposite of a model prisoner. Even in his remaining few days of freedom before reporting to prison, Tyson could not keep from crossing the law. Prior to surrendering to authorities, the boxer received a speeding ticket in Ohio. After he began his prison sentence, Tyson violated prison procedures, incurring punishment from the warden.[5]

Mike Tyson's case is significant in that it is the most visible instance of an athlete committing a sex crime. However, the boxer is only one of many athletes similarly charged. Some fifteen alleged gang rapes involving about fifty athletes were reported between June 1989 and June 1990, according to *Mademoiselle* magazine.

What disturbs law-enforcement officials is that the reported crimes may be just the tip of the iceberg. For example, only about 5 percent of gang rapes are ever reported to authorities, says *USA Today*. Furthermore, a Towson State University study in 1990 found that athletes were far more likely to admit being involved in date rape than were nonathletes on campus.[6]

Sex scandals involving athletes have occurred with disturbing regularity in recent years. Sexual assault charges have been reported at St. John's University in New York, the University of Wyoming, Kentucky State University, and the University of California-Berkeley. In 1991, Ian Dale, an Arizona State basketball player, pleaded guilty to attempted sexual abuse and assault. He was put on probation for three years.[7]

Charges of gang rape have been levied against players on many professional teams, including the New York Mets, Washington Capitals, and Cincinnati Bengals. In a civil suit against the Bengals, a woman identified only as "Victoria C" charged that Cincinnati was negligent because it did not control its players, leading to conditions that she says made it possible for her to be brutally gang-raped.[8] Even when charges against players are dropped, as occurred in the case against the Mets players, a stigma remains and the reputations of the accuser and accused are never completely restored.

Tyson was not the only boxer to forfeit his boxing career after a conviction for a sex crime. A few months before Tony Ayala, Jr., was scheduled to box Davey Moore for the WBA junior middleweight championship, a New Jersey jury convicted Ayala of rape and other charges. He assaulted a woman on New Year's Day, 1983, and received a prison sentence of thirty-five years.

One reason so many athletes find themselves in court is because many of them tend to dismiss the enormous consequences of rape, contends Dr. Claire Walsh, a researcher on gang rape and director of the Campus and Community Consultation Service in St. Augustine, Florida. They seem to think that they've done nothing to harm the women they attack, when in fact, rape "is a traumatizing event that changes the life of the victim." Dr. Walsh says a third of all rape victims consider suicide.[9]

Rape is not a product of natural sexual urges, says Dr. Walsh. When an athlete (or anyone else) rapes, it is because of his desire to dominate or humiliate his victim. He gets his way by intimidation and brute force, she says.[10]

Another problem with athletes is that they've come to feel that they are somehow entitled to sex, said Ed Gondolf, the author of *Man Against Woman: What Every Woman Should Know About Violent Men*. Rapists commonly feel, " 'I deserve this, and the way I get what I want is to take it,' " Gondolf said.[11]

When a group of athletes rapes a single woman, the men are showing the worst side of male bonding and group behavior, says Dr. Walsh. "It tells you something about the power of peer pressure and the need to have status within the group, the need to score," she says.[12]

According to her research, there is a tendency for so-called rape-prone men to be members of aggressive team sports. She cites one study in which college football and basketball players allegedly committed a third more sexual assaults than did any comparable group of college males. Such men are more "tolerant of rape, sexually coercive," and tend to think of sexual assaults merely as exhibitions of manliness. An athlete tends to think a rape victim got what she deserved, found Dr. Walsh.[13]

Athletes may also be prone to sexual assault because they've been given preferential treatment much of their lives due to their athletic accomplishments. The best athletes early in life are "idolized, afforded privileged positions, and provided favors," said Dr. Walsh.[14]

Many attacks by college athletes have taken

place in the posh special dormitories provided by some athletic departments. In February 1989, police arrested several University of Oklahoma football players on charges of gang-raping a young woman. The attack took place in the athletes' dormitory. Two men were convicted. The twenty-year-old woman was leaving a bathroom when her attackers grabbed her. The men brutally raped her four times, holding hands over her mouth to silence her screams. Investigators displayed a bloodstained rug as evidence of the savagery of the attack. When two Oklahoma football players who were witnesses gave statements to the police, they were intimidated by the accused rapists. "My cousins from Detroit will come down and take care of you," one witness was told.[15]

Nigel Clay, a rapist convicted in the case, still maintains from his jail cell that he was innocent, but he doesn't deny that he received preferential treatment from the University of Oklahoma. His admission is important because it says that universities may unwittingly be setting up an atmosphere of tolerance for antisocial behavior that leads male athletes to believe they can get away with acts of violence against women. Some of the things Clay says he received were gifts, sums of money (including an $800 payment), and the temporary use of a Mercedes-Benz. He admits lying to NCAA investigators about the gifts to protect his school.[16]

An athlete's coach may try to cover up a sex crime. For example, in 1983, then–University of Maryland basketball coach Lefty Driesell tried to protect star forward Herman Veal. Driesell put pressure on a female student to rescind sexual misconduct charges against Veal, reported *Sports Illustrated*. Instead of capitulating, the victim filed harassment charges against the coach. He received an official reprimand from Maryland authorities.

The punishment may have been insufficient, because shortly thereafter Driesell found himself in trouble for interfering in a police investigation into the death of Maryland basketball player Len Bias from a cocaine overdose.[17]

Another male-female issue that has drawn widespread public attention in recent years is that of sexual harassment suffered by women reporters assigned to interview male athletes in locker rooms. One incident involved Boston newspaper reporter Lisa Olson. Three members of the New England Patriots cornered Olson as she interviewed one player. Allegedly, the three verbally assaulted her with obscene comments and gestures. The three players were naked as they allegedly harassed her.

Instead of apologizing to Olson and reprimanding the Patriot players, then team owner Victor Kiam came to their defense. He was overheard using a sexist term to describe Olson and in effect blamed the victim for the problem. Fans also supported the players. They sent the reporter disgusting letters and cursed her from the stands whenever she covered New England games. To his credit, NFL commissioner Paul Tagliabue took Olson's charges seriously. He fined Zeke Mowatt, one of the players involved, $12,500 for his role in the affair. (Subsequently, Mowatt was released by the Patriots for reasons unrelated to the harassment of Olson.)[18]

Although Olson reached a modest financial settlement with the Patriots, she lost her career. Convinced that a woman could not be treated fairly when covering male sporting events, she moved to Australia.[19]

In 1992, another sexual harassment case emerged. University of Alabama administrative assistant Nancy Watts filed a suit in federal court, charging that her boss, basketball coach Wimp

Boston Herald *sports reporter Lisa Olson after the National Football League's decision to impose fines for an incident in which Olson was sexually harassed in the Patriots' locker room.*

Sanderson, hit her during a heated argument. Watts said that Sanderson lost his temper when she brought up the name of another employee with whom the coach allegedly had had an affair. The beleaguered coach resigned under pressure, claiming in his defense that Watts was hysterical and suffered a black eye when she ran into his outstretched hand. Also included in Watts's suit were the university and athletic director Hootie Ingram.[20]

The problems of society at large are reflected in sports scandals. Athletes, despite their strength and stamina, have learned that they are not immune to the HIV virus, an infection that doctors say can lead to serious AIDS-related illnesses.

A sad milestone in the occurrence of the HIV virus was thirty-two-year-old Earvin "Magic" Johnson's 1991 admission that he had tested positive. (Tennis great Arthur Ashe, who died of AIDS in 1993, announced in 1992 that he too had contracted AIDS, but his was probably nonsexual, received from a blood transfusion during a heart bypass operation in 1983.) Johnson admitted that he had contracted the disease from promiscuous heterosexual behavior. While some fans and writers praised the athlete for his honesty and openness, others attacked him. Many said that his HIV infection made him less than a hero in their eyes. For example, major league pitcher Nolan Ryan, in his 1992 autobiography *Miracle Man,* wrote, "I have a problem with making a hero out of him because of AIDS." Ryan said that Johnson was foolhardy for persisting in risky sexual behavior.[21]

Others disagreed, saying that Johnson's disease should not detract from all the charity work he has done. "When a hero like Magic Johnson tests HIV positive, it is an all-too-powerful reminder of each person's vulnerability and drives home the impor-

Earvin "Magic" Johnson weeps during a ceremony to retire his Los Angeles Lakers jersey. Johnson retired from basketball after testing positive for human immunodeficiency virus (HIV), which causes AIDS.

tant link between education and survival," said William H. Gray, the president of the United Negro College Fund, for which Johnson has helped raise $6.5 million.[22]

While Johnson is the most famous, he is not the only athlete to contract the virus. Several stars from a variety of sports have already died of AIDS-related complications.

In 1986, forty-three-year-old Jerry Smith, a former tight end for the Washington Redskins for twelve years, died from complications due to the disease. A member of the 1968 Olympic decathlon team, Thomas Waddell, died in 1987. A former lightweight boxer, Esteban DeJesus, died in 1989. NASCAR stock car driver Tim Richmond succumbed to AIDS at thirty-four, in 1989. Former major league baseball player Alan Wiggins, thirty-two, died of AIDS in 1991.[23]

Basketball superstar Charles Barkley predicted that Magic Johnson's announcement was merely the first in a wave of future HIV infections because of the promiscuous life-styles that some athletes lead. "If no one [else] does, it'll be a miracle," said Barkley. "There are an awful lot of men ... sweating it out in this league," he said. "If you don't have it now, you should never have it. If you don't practice safe sex after being scared like this, you're out of your mind."[24]

Barkley's reference was to those athletes who flirt with HIV infection by having sex with a multitude of the fans who pursue them. Many players even "share" sexual partners when female "groupies" show up at the team's hotel. Barkley noted that other NBA players feared they might contract the disease if they also had sex with whomever infected Magic Johnson, as well as with any women he may have given the infection to. "About five or six other players are puking in the sinks right now, what with the way some of these guys share women," said Magic Johnson's former agent, George Andrews.[25]

Some columnists challenged Johnson's veracity. Writer Dave Kindred of the *Sporting News* said in an October 1992 issue that he didn't believe the player's story, saying he thought it more likely that Johnson had received the infection from sharing needles with a drug user or from unprotected homosexual sex. Johnson denied such allegations. He maintained that he became HIV positive because he had been promiscuous with many women.

Another athletic star who got in trouble for taking his sexual behavior to extremes was third baseman Wade Boggs of the Boston Red Sox. Although Boggs was married, he was unfaithful to his wife with Margo Adams, who had dated many other players. The woman revealed the story of her affair with Boggs in *Penthouse,* and most newspapers covered her allegations. The third baseman admitted the affair, saying in his defense "that a disease was overtaking Wade Boggs." He said that he suffered from sex addiction.[26]

Another married player to suffer the embarrassment of being caught in a sex scandal was basketball player James Worthy. The star of the Los Angeles Lakers was arrested on November 15, 1990, for soliciting prostitution from two female undercover officers. He was given one year's probation, made to perform forty hours of community service, and fined $500.[27]

Worthy previously had enjoyed an excellent reputation as a role model for his young fans. So too had former star baseball player Steve Garvey until he involved himself in a messy series of relationships that earned him the reputation of an insatiable womanizer. Garvey lost his dream of entering politics after he had been involved in three serious relationships simultaneously, impregnating two of the women. As soon as these revelations surfaced, Margo Adams listed Garvey as one of her lovers in the aforementioned *Penthouse* article.[28]

Had Boggs, Worthy, and Garvey played sports in an earlier era, their sexual misadventures might have been covered up. Sportswriters used to protect the reputations of players because many of them drew salaries from the teams they covered for performing various public-relations duties. Others idolized the players they covered.

Babe Ruth, the New York Yankees slugger, was one such player protected during his lifetime by the press. By all biographical accounts, Ruth had an enormous appetite for women, food, and alcohol. He once claimed to have had sex with every woman in a St. Louis house of prostitution in a single night. The married Ruth often brought two women at a time to his hotel room. "One woman couldn't satisfy him," recalled sportswriter Fred Lieb.[29]

During the 1960s, another athlete imitated Ruth's life-style, although he lacked his talent on a baseball diamond. Pitcher Bo Belinsky made headlines for romantic escapades. Belinsky told the press what it was like to date the most famous Hollywood stars of the day, including Ann-Margaret, Tina Louise, Paulette Goddard, Connie Stevens, and Juliet Prowse. He ended up marrying and then divorcing a *Playboy* centerfold.[30]

But Belinsky's exploits paled in comparison to an incident in 1973, in which New York Yankee pitchers Fritz Peterson and Mike Kekich had what they called a "life swap." They literally exchanged children, cars, dogs, and wives. When the news hit every publication from *Ladies Home Journal* to the staid *New York Times,* Major League Baseball was horribly embarrassed. Religious groups refused to attend Yankee games until baseball commissioner Bowie Kuhn apologized to the youth of America.

For their part, the two couples insisted that they had done nothing wrong. Peterson married Kekich's wife, Susan, while Kekich and Peterson's wife, Marilyn, lived together until they found they were incompatible. "We were attracted to each other and we fell in love," Susan said. The furor ended a few years later, when both players left the major leagues.[31]

Professional sports have also survived scandals in which sports figures admitted that they were gay.

Even as homosexuals have fought and sued for their civil rights, the world of sports has shown little or no tolerance. In 1980, for example, Oakland A's outfielder Glenn Burke was dropped from the roster by manager Billy Martin after a newspaper article referred to an unnamed gay player. According to Burke, Martin said he didn't want a homosexual playing for him.[32]

In 1988, umpire Dave Pallone was also dismissed after ten years in the National League when his gay status became public. "Baseball ripped out my heart and soul, just so they might eliminate what they felt would be adverse publicity," said Pallone.[33]

After he was fired, Pallone said that a dozen pro baseball players had kept their homosexuality hidden for fear that they too would be driven from the game. The former umpire said that those most hurt by homophobia in sports are young gay men and women who desperately seek positive gay role models to emulate. "They are in desperate search for the athlete they may look up to, knowing [the gay athletes] have made it in pro sports regardless of their sexuality," he said.[34]

While the majority of coaches who discriminate

The National League dismissed umpire Dave Pallone in 1988, when it was revealed he was gay. He said he knew of many professional athletes who kept their homosexuality a secret for fear of discrimination.

against athletes on the basis of sexual preference do so subtly, head women's basketball coach Renée Portland of Pennsylvania State University drew national headlines in 1991, when she openly objected to having lesbians play for her. Embarrassed Penn State administrators insisted that the university would condone no discrimination on the basis of sexual preference, but if Portland was rebuked for her conduct, the university did so privately.[35]

For many years, officials in all major sports simply denied that any of their players could be gay. And newspaper reporters of the 1920s and 1930s refused to print stories about an athlete's sexuality that might embarrass the sport. For that reason, one of history's greatest tennis players, Bill Tilden, was able to keep the secret of his homosexuality away from fans even as fellow athletes ostracized him in private.[36]

Players maintain that there's another side to sex scandals in sports, saying that being a star athlete means having fans of the opposite sex throw themselves at you. Players fear that they might be set up and charged with a sex crime because the accuser seeks notoriety, money, revenge, or all three.

Once an athlete has been charged with a sex crime he is stigmatized. A case in point during the 1991–1992 basketball season involved All-American senior Todd Day and three University of Arkansas teammates who had group sex with a thirty-four-year-old woman in an athletic dormitory. The woman claimed that she had been raped; the players claimed they had had her permission before proceeding to have sex. A police investigation found insufficient evidence to file charges, although the school suspended the four players for one month.[37]

Day claimed innocence and said that he felt like

a victim even though he had acquired no criminal record. He received hate mail, much of it calculated to wound him. One man sent a photo of Day speaking to a class of students. The player's face was scrawled over. "The note was from a man who said I was a disgrace to Arkansas basketball and that he hoped his son never grew up to be like me."[38]

Athletes need to learn an important lesson from Day's predicament, said Arkansas basketball coach Nolan Richardson. Players in the public eye must realize that there are serious consequences when they fail to be discreet. "As hard as the whole thing was ... it made him grow up some," he said about Day. "He understands more about taking responsibility for his actions and not acting on impulse ... because he's in the public eye."[39]

And like it or not, today's press not only refuses to coddle athletes, it also strips them of the rights and privileges that ordinary citizens have. Day was not the only athlete to be tried and found guilty in the press, only to be vindicated by the legal process. A good example is the accusation of rape that hung over Dwight Gooden, Vince Coleman, and Daryl Boston in the spring of 1992. Many newspapers reported that they were suspects even though no charges were ever brought against them. Athletes need to realize that today's lack of judgment is tomorrow's headline.[40]

This was tragically true of Dodgers relief pitcher Hugh Casey, the hero of the 1948 World Series, who in 1949 was judged to be the father of a child in a patrimony suit. His career in tatters, his marriage shattered, Casey made a phone call to his estranged wife on July 3, 1950. "So help me, God, I'm innocent of that charge," he told her. Those were his last words. He killed himself while on the phone.[41]

Many years earlier, in 1894, another unfortunate episode occurred involving Baltimore Orioles pitcher Edgar McNabb. The athlete had an affair with the wife of the Pacific Northwest Baseball League's ex-president, Mrs. E. E. Rockwell, an actress known by her stage pseudonym of Louise Kellogg. When the actress ended the relationship, McNabb killed her and himself.[42]

Another failed affair also resulted in the 1907 suicide of Chick Stahl, manager of the American League Boston Puritans. Although Stahl was married only a few months before his death, another woman announced that he had gotten her pregnant and would have to marry her. Mortified, Stahl committed suicide in an Indiana hotel room, and his wife died the following year of alcohol poisoning.[43]

Some athletic coaches have had affairs with the wives of their assistant coaches. While football coach at Oklahoma, Barry Switzer allegedly became involved with the wife of his assistant head coach, Larry Lacewell. Humiliated, Lacewell felt he had no choice but to resign, according to a published account by Howard Cosell. In a similar episode, Cornell University fired Coach Maxie Baughan for having an affair with the spouse of one of his assistants.[44]

Coaches have also had affairs with female college students. According to sportscaster Howard Cosell, married head football coach Sonny Randle had an affair with a coed at the University of Virginia. Cosell also called basketball coach Tates Locke a coed-chaser when the latter coached at Clemson.[45]

One case that made national headlines in 1992 was the arrest of twenty-seven-year-old Peter Anding, a writer who covered high school sports for the *Chicago Sun-Times*. He had allegedly written favorable stories about athletes in exchange for sex. He was charged with aggravated criminal sexual assault and the manufacture of child pornography after allegedly filming many of the athletes. A spokesman said Anding admitted involvement in approximately 150 encounters.[46]

7

CHEATING TO WIN

Not even Little League baseball is safe from controversy. In 1992, the Zamboanga team from the Philippines won the Little League World Series. An investigation, however, determined that the coach had used eight illegal players. The eight were not original members of the team but had been recruited from other teams outside the city of Zamboanga, in violation of Little League rules. To make way for the eight, eight members of the original team had been removed from the squad. And several members of the team were supposedly older than the maximum of twelve years of age.

The Filipinos had won the title by beating Long Beach (California) Little League 15–4 on August 29. The title reverted back to Long Beach on a 6–0 forfeit after a ruling by the International Tournament Committee for Little League Baseball, Inc.

A U.S. Little League administrator, Bob McKittrick, said that two groups of boys were cheated by Filipino officials. In addition to the Long Beach team, he said that "the kids who were left off the Philippines team were cheated too [because] they might have won it legally."[1]

Cheating may be as old as sport itself. In the ancient Olympic Games, a boxer named Eupolus wanted to win so much that he bribed three fellow boxers to lie down during their matches with him.[2]

In the days before professional sports earned national attention, and athletes became known from coast to coast, many athletes cheated by playing both professional and college ball. Many of these players wanted the best of both worlds. They wanted to preserve their amateur status and earn a college degree, but they also wanted to earn quick money for playing pro ball. In 1992, the Society for American Baseball Research determined that a Yale baseball player, Alexander Brown Nevin, also played for a professional team called the Elizabeth Resolutes under the name of "Nevins."[3]

During the 1920s, college football players, to protect their eligibility, routinely cheated by playing professional football under false identities. One of those bitterly opposed to this practice was Amos Alonzo Stagg, then the coach of the University of Chicago, who won 314 games during his career.

"Under the guise of fair play but countenancing rank dishonesty in playing men under assumed names, scores of professional teams have sprung up in the last two or three years," complained Stagg in 1923. "These teams are bidding hard for college players in order to capitalize not only on their ability but also and mostly on the name of the college they come from."[4]

A major part of the problem was the fact that large amounts of money were being gambled on these games. Coaches like Stagg were concerned that college players would be tempted to throw games or shave points because of their association with gamblers. One popular story has it that when players from Notre Dame and the University of Illinois played in the Carlinville-Taylorville professional game in 1921, the First National Bank, on losing to Carlinville, had to move to Taylorville to satisfy a bet. While most of the players were not punished by their schools for playing in the game, a few were. Joey Sternaman, later a fine professional football player with Chicago, was the best-known player to be thrown off the Illinois squad for his involvement.[5]

Years later, in 1991, another type of scandal rocked Auburn University, the perennial Alabama football power under head coach Pat Dye. Dye resigned under pressure as athletic director and coach after former player Eric Ramsey released secretly made tapes that revealed serious improprieties in the Tigers' program. The tapes revealed that Ramsey had asked for, and gotten, illegal payments and a bank loan, both serious NCAA rules violations. Dye and his staff came across as less than responsible educators. The student, however, was not innocent. On tape after tape, he was the one who had solicited improperly from Auburn's football staff.

Too many colleges treat cheating as if it were a trivial offense. After University of Oklahoma wrestler Joe Brett Reynolds was expelled from school for a minimum of two years on charges of academic fraud (another student had taken a final exam for him), he appealed to the board of regents. Rejecting the advice of the school's then-president, the board reduced the suspension. One board member even suggested that perhaps Reynold's professor was guilty of entrapment, said *Sports Illustrated*.[6]

Some boxing matches have been fixed, although these are usually such behind-the-scenes dealings that it is generally impossible to prove that one or both fighters threw a fight. An exception occurred in

1906, when lightweight boxing champion Joe Gans admitted fixing matches with Jimmy Britt and Terry McGovern for money—a scandal that had the boxing world in an uproar for years.[7] Another famous fix was admitted to by middleweight boxer Jake LaMotta, who threw a fight to boxer Billy Fox.[8]

In 1964, in the first Cassius Clay (later to change his name to Muhammad Ali) versus Sonny Liston fight, the defending champion Liston began to realize that his young, swift opponent would prevail. To get an edge, Liston ordered a trainer to rub an astringent compound on his gloves. For two rounds, young Clay was blinded and ran around the ring, literally running for his life. At one point he wanted to concede, but his trainer refused to let him quit. In the sixth round, Clay's eyes cleared up. Liston's cheating had only gained him a bit more time before Clay defeated him.[9]

An often disputed case was the claim by Jack Dempsey's former manager, a man named Kearns, that he had unfairly "loaded" the fighter's hand tapes with a substance that turned as hard as a rock when wet with sweat. Dempsey supposedly had this unfair advantage in his first fight, in 1919, when he nearly killed defending champion Jess Willard. The challenger broke Willard's jaw, knocked out six teeth, closed an eye, and did other bodily and internal damage. Many fans watching the fight feared that Dempsey *would* kill Willard.[10]

Baseball is another sport in which allegations of cheating are frequently made. Pitchers who cheat do so by scuffing balls with emery boards or sandpaper, and by applying illegal substances such as petroleum jelly or saliva. Some batters bore holes in the end of bats and cork them, thereby adding both distance and speed to their hits. "People have been trying to get an edge for as long as baseball's been

A 1965 heavyweight title match between Muhammad Ali (then Cassius Clay) and Sonny Liston.

played," said pitcher Ron Darling. "It's part of the lore." Former New York Mets manager George Bamberger (and a longtime pitching coach) estimated that half of all pitchers use an illegal pitch now and then.[11]

One of the most notorious incidents of cheating was the time umpires caught Minnesota's Joe Niekro trying to toss away the incriminating sandpaper and emery board he had in his possession—while millions watched the nationally televised game in 1987. Niekro was suspended for ten days.

Some pitchers openly admit using scuffed balls. Kevin Gross, the former Phillies pitcher, said that he used a ball that had first been scuffed by a rival pitcher. "I threw some of my best pitches using that ball he left," said Gross.[12]

Gaylord Perry, now in the Baseball Hall of Fame, liked to joke about doctoring baseballs, figuring he'd gain a psychological edge over opponents who might fear what he was throwing. He confessed in his autobiography, *Me and the Spitter,* that early in his career he had often thrown an illegal pitch. "I reckon I tried everything on the old apple [baseball] but salt and pepper and chocolate sauce toppin'," said Perry.

One time, when playing against a team managed by Billy Martin, he smeared K-Y Jelly on the ball. The feisty Martin asked umpire Bill Kunkel to take a whiff of the ball, but the ump said allergies and a deviated septum had destroyed his sniffing ability. "I got an umpire who can't see or smell," groaned Martin.[13]

Other well-known pitchers who cheated were Whitey Ford (scuffing balls with his wedding ring), Rick Honeycutt (sandpaper in his glove), Lew Burdette and Preacher Roe (saliva on the ball), and Clyde King (bubble gum on the ball).[14]

Corked bats are hard to detect except by using X rays. Nonetheless, many players have admitted using them, making such announcements *after* they had retired. Slugger Norm Cash added not a few extra-base hits to his total with a corked bat, as did Graig Nettles. Sportswriter Peter Gammons estimated that as many as one out of five hitters may use corked bats.[15]

Old-time ballplayers cheated as much as do ballplayers today. One of the illegal tricks performed by Connie Mack, a catcher in the nineteenth century (later to become a Hall of Fame manager), was to use his glove to "tip" a batter's bat when he swung. This always slowed the swing down enough so that if a batter should connect with the ball, he did so with little power. "Why, I just help the hitters hit the ball, that's all," was Mack's wry excuse.[16]

Even tennis players try to gain an illegal edge. A case in point was a 1983 scandal in which Southern Illinois University allowed tennis stars Ken Flach and Robert Seguso to play even though they had all but abandoned their studies, making them scholastically ineligible. "All we did was play tennis and eat pizza," admitted Flach. The two led the school to Division II national championships from 1981 to 1983, until university administrators finally cleaned house. In the aftermath, Southern Illinois reassigned athletic director Ed Bingham and dropped tennis for three years.[17]

One of the most violated rules in tennis is the prohibition against a player getting signals from a coach during a match. "We all signaled," said Vitas Gerulaitis's coach, Fred Stolle. "I might touch my nose or scratch my ear to tell Vitas to go to the backhand on an approach."[18]

Boris Becker's coach, Ion Tiriac, used a cigarette to send smoke signals to his player during the serve. Steffi Graf was once penalized when her father was caught signaling some tips on strategy to her.[19]

Some cases of cheating are so bizarre that they bring national laughter instead of outrage when the perpetrator is caught. In 1980, race fans thought that a twenty-six-year-old administrative assistant named Rosie Ruiz won the Boston Marathon, only to learn that she had not run the entire course. With the aid of an accomplice, she allegedly started the course, dropped out, and rejoined the race near the end of the track. Following an investigation, a friend said that Ruiz had pulled a similar stunt to finish respectably in the New York Marathon by dropping out and taking a subway to the finish line.[20]

Her credibility dropped even further when it was revealed that her promoter, Steve Marek, had been forbidden to run in the 1979 New York Marathon for "falsifying his own entry form," according to *Newsweek* writer Pete Axthelm. Ruiz's brief moments of glory became a nightmare when she first became a national disgrace and then the butt of many talk show jokes.[21]

Cheating has become almost a routine problem with the America's Cup race, the world's most famous yacht race. It is so common that it is an almost accepted part of strategy, and strong security is a must for the international competitors who try to win the treasured trophy cup.

One of the most embarrassing cheating incidents in Cup history occurred in July 1983, when two members of the *Canada I* team were spotted in diving gear trying to take pictures of the *Australia II*. One of them, Jim Johnston, was arrested by police. The Australians magnanimously dropped charges against him, but his underwater camera and film were confiscated.[22]

In 1986, the *America II* team showed its integrity when they informed the Royal Thames Yacht Club that they had been offered secret plans of the British *Crusader*'s keel for $25,000. Police arrested a worker at the foundry that had cast the keel. Australian cynics said they doubted the crew would have turned down plans for the far more competitive *Australia III* had they been available.[23]

As a result of such shenanigans, security for all America's Cup entries rivaled that of the White House. Closed-circuit TV monitors kept tabs on all who entered the complex. The New Zealand entry not only put up sturdy fencing, but it also had barbed wire on top of the fencing. Security guards threatened to outnumber crew members. And in the case of Australia, all crew members—even skipper Iain Murray—volunteered for security guard duty.[24]

In recent years, World Cup soccer has also had problems with cheating. A professional goalie from Chile staged an injury from a firecracker blast and blamed it on an opposing team, hoping to win a forfeit. Instead, Chile was ruled ineligible for world play, reported the *New York Times*. Similarly, World Cup officials ruled Mexico ineligible after that country falsified the ages of players competing in a youth tournament.[25]

Cheating has also surfaced in the world of sports agents as the chief negotiators for athletes. Most unscrupulous agents never get caught, but agents Norby Walters and Lloyd Bloom were. Convicted of conspiracy, extortion, and fraud in 1989, the two men received, respectively, five- and three-year jail sentences, plus $250,000 and $145,000 fines. Walters also received an additional eighteen months in prison for mail fraud. The agents had illegally signed at least forty-three football players to binding contracts, getting the jump on honest agents

Sports agents Norby Walters (above left) and Lloyd Bloom (below left) were convicted in 1989 on charges that they illegally signed college football players to contracts before their college careers were over.

who had to wait until the athletes were no longer eligible to play under NCAA rules. Walters and Bloom used a Mafia connection to intimidate players who later wanted out of their signed contracts. The Mafia captain, Michael Franzese, actually owned part of the crooked agents' agency.[26]

The NCAA rule is easy to understand, stating that "An individual shall be ineligible for participation in an intercollegiate sport if he or she has agreed (orally or in writing) to be represented by an agent for the purpose of marketing his or her athletics ability or reputation in that sport." Nonetheless, agents Walters and Bloom managed to sign some of the finest young college athletes to illegal contracts, including the University of Iowa's powerful running back Ronnie Harmon and Temple University running back Paul Palmer, who finished second in the 1986 Heisman Trophy ballot.[27]

These players were not alone. Former University of Nebraska Heisman Trophy–winning running back Mike Rozier admitted accepting a $2,400 payoff from a representative of agent Mike Trope.[28] And while at the University of North Carolina, superstar linebacker Lawrence Taylor prematurely signed contracts with so many sports agents that he had to take out a loan to pay them back or risk losing his eligibility, says agent James J. Kiles III, who helped Taylor obtain the loan.[29]

Why do such abuses occur? For one thing, competition is fierce. One recent estimate by the Sports Lawyers Association is that agents outnumber professional athletes three to one.[30] Therefore, to gain an edge, some agents have few qualms about offering first-round basketball and football players under-the-table inducements. "I saw a lot of guys flown around in Lear jets [and] given women, cars and cash," said football player Tim Green, a former first-round pick in the NFL draft.[31]

Getting rid of cheating agents is difficult, but some measures have been taken. Both Major League Baseball and the National Football League Players Association have tried to weed out dishonest agents by making it more difficult to obtain certification as an agent. Fifteen states have introduced legislation to keep agents in line, and there is a movement to introduce federal legislation.[32]

Occasionally scandals involve executives at the highest level of sport. In December 1992, such a scandal rocked the U.S. Olympic Committee. The USOC president, Robert Helmick, resigned after *USA Today* revealed that he had received more than $450,000 for legal work with individuals and companies that had Olympic ties (or were seeking Olympic ties). After the USOC determined that Helmick had violated its conflict-of-interest policies, the president resigned his lifetime appointment, still denying that he had done anything wrong. According to a member of the three-person International Olympic Committee investigating the allegations against Helmick, "dismissal" was one possible action it could have taken. The fifty-four-year-old Helmick's decision to relinquish his title ended the matter.[33]

8

OUT-OF-CONTROL FANS

Some fans simply aren't satisfied with watching their heroes from a grandstand seat. Some go to bizarre and even terrifying lengths to mingle with their heroes.

In 1932, one woman decided that if she couldn't have Chicago Cubs' shortstop Billy Jurges for her own, then no one else would. She went after him with a gun. Fortunately for Jurges, her aim was off, and he suffered only a minor flesh wound.[1]

A similar incident involved Ruth Ann Steinhagen, a young woman who became infatuated with Philadelphia Phillies first baseman Eddie Waitkus. In 1949, Steinhagen took a room in a Chicago hotel when the Phillies were scheduled to play the Cubs. She sent the ballplayer a note through a bellboy to invite him to her room. Assuming Steinhagen had romance in mind, Waitkus complied.[2]

Waitkus knocked and entered, taking a chair. But by way of greeting him, the nineteen-year-old woman leveled the barrel of a rifle on him. She told him that she'd been obsessed with him for two years and that now he was to die. She shot him through the chest but found that she was unable to kill herself as she had planned. She called the front desk for medical assistance. The critically wounded Waitkus not only survived, but played the next year for the National League's pennant-winning Phillies.[3]

Steinhagen was mentally ill and was committed to a mental hospital for three years. "I just became nuttier and nuttier about the guy," she admitted to police. Feeling that a relationship with him was impossible, she decided to destroy him. The incident was the model for the shooting of Roy Hobbs, the hero of *The Natural,* the novel by Bernard Malamud.[4]

Jurges and Waitkus were not the only athletes to be stalked by a besotted fan. And not only male athletes are affected. Sometimes a male fan becomes irrationally obsessed. In June 1992, a paranoid-schizophrenic California man who had harassed German Olympic skating champion Katarina Witt was sent to a mental institution for thirty-seven months. The man, forty-seven-year-old Harry Veltman III, believed that Witt would return his ardor and had sent her nude photographs of himself and sexually explicit letters.

In actions frighteningly reminiscent of the Waitkus-Steinhagen affair, the fan told Witt that he planned to kill himself, and had given her thinly veiled threats. "You would rather die than live without me!" he wrote her.[5]

Such actions by fans are difficult to control. As a result, all professional sports have had to step up security to protect athletes from those who think the price of admission gives them additional liberties. In the very first professional game, the Cincinnati Red Stockings versus the Brooklyn Atlantics on June 14, 1870, a fan supposedly leaped on the back of Cincinnati outfielder Cal McVey as he attempted to make a catch. In April 1907, the hometown Giants forfeited opening day when fans bombarded visiting Philadelphia with snowballs. During the 1934 World Series, hometown Detroit fans showered St. Louis's Joe Medwick with so much trash and fruit that he had to leave the game.[6]

Even umpires are sometimes attacked by fans. In 1940, fan Frank Germano received a six-month jail sentence for assaulting umpire George Magerkurth in Brooklyn's Ebbets Field. And in 1981, a crazed New York Yankee fan rushed out of his seat in Yankee Stadium to attack Mike Reilly.[7]

Confrontations arise when thin-skinned ballplayers are not content to let insults go. In 1912, for example, according to the *New York Times* Detroit's Ty Cobb jumped into the stands during a game against New York and both hit and kicked a fan who had relentlessly razzed him. "Jabs bounded off the spectator's face like a golf ball from a rock," the *Times* reported. Although Cobb saw that the fan had lost one hand and most of the other in a factory accident, the player continued to beat him. When Cobb was suspended, his teammates protested by refusing to play in a game the next day.[8]

Slugger Babe Ruth also once vaulted into the stands to try to assault a heckler. The fan, fortunately for his face and the Babe's career, managed to flee. Ruth was suspended for one game, and the American League punished him by saying that he no longer could be captain of the Yankees—an honor he had held for only six games.[9]

Fed up with what they perceive to be fan abuse, many players overreact. In 1991, recovering alcoholic Albert Belle of the Cleveland Indians fired a baseball from point-blank range into the chest of a fan who had suggested he come to his house for a keg party. The American League suspended the player for one week minus pay. That same year, Jose Canseco had to be restrained by his manager from assaulting a fan who had made suggestive comments about the player's friendship with the singer Madonna. In 1990, Luis Polonia hit a fan who brought up the player's conviction for having sex with an underage girl. In 1990, the nation's National Association of Intercollegiate Athletics (NAIA) leading rusher, Marlo Johnson of Mesa State College, responded to something a fan said by breaking the man's jaw with his helmet. Johnson was arrested on third-degree battery charges and was suspended for the 1990 play-offs.[10]

When fans throw ice, bottles, and other debris at players, it is inevitable that some athletes will retaliate. After Florida State fans in November 1991 abused him verbally and physically with ice chunks, Miami Hurricanes defensive lineman Mark Caesar threw a cup of ice water into the stands. The water soaked a security guard, and Caesar was arrested for simple battery.[11]

What is happening, say sports psychologists, is that the sports world is a microcosm of what is happening in the so-called real world. "We live in a more hostile time," says University of Southern California behavioral psychologist Chaytor Mason. "We're expressing ourselves in ways we didn't used to. Before World War II we were nice."[12]

Another possibility is that the multimillion-dollar salaries of today's players tend to raise the hackles of ordinary citizens who see themselves as downtrodden souls trying to scrape enough together for food and shelter. "Here's a hero out there, and he's probably not going to attack you, and you can humiliate him, defeat him verbally," says University of Pennsylvania psychology professor Alan Fiske. "It's a peculiar way of defeating a person of high status."[13]

Sports Illustrated writer Nicholas Dawidoff thinks the problem may be that fans know far more scandalous material about athletes than did fans of past decades. Where once sportswriters had a chummy relationship with players, they now are adversaries, looking for the next scoop to make tomorrow's sports headline. As a result, only a handful of today's players have on- and off-field lives that qualify them as heroes in the public's perception. If the press gave similar scrutiny to the lives of players during the so-called Golden Age of Sport, players such as Babe Ruth, Leo Durocher, and Dizzy Dean would no doubt have been vilified in their day. "Television, the print media, and talk shows examine every minor detail of a player's life," said Boston Bruins coach Mike Milbury. "There used to be some sort of sanctity."[14]

While most fans come to sporting events to cheer their teams, a few have another agenda—to heckle players to distraction. So rowdy were fans in Madison Square Garden in 1990–91, that 359 of them were ejected during New York professional basketball and hockey games. During the NBA playoffs in 1992, Chicago fans, unable to get to Portland center Kevin Duckworth, verbally abused his mother. One fan even poured a beer on her.[15]

In 1973, when the Cincinnati Reds were playing the Mets in New York's Shea Stadium, fans deliberately went after Reds players and their wives. The game had to be stopped to rescue the wives, who were being insulted and threatened with assault on the third-base side of the stadium. On the first-base side, fans contented themselves with tearing down a barrier separating them from then-Cincinnati manager Sparky Anderson so that they could spit in his direction. When outfielder Pete Rose of the Reds went back against the warning track to try to catch a long ball off Tom Seaver's bat, a fan doused him with beer. After the game, players raced for safety as fans stormed the infield, carting away home plate and bits of sod.[16]

"Can you imagine, in the United States of America, going through something like this?" a bewildered Anderson asked. "It just shows you what's happening in this country."[17]

Things had not changed nineteen years later. In 1992, in his first appearance in Pittsburgh in a Mets uniform since leaving the Pirates for a $29 million, five-year contract with New York, slugger Bobby Bonilla was rudely and dangerously treated by fans. He was hit with coins and rubber balls, then had to put on a batting helmet when someone walloped him with a golf ball. "I didn't know what to expect coming back, but throwing things?" said Bonilla. "You never expect that."[18]

Football coaches are also the target of fans' anger. In spite of the fact that he had won 69 percent of his games and ran a clean program, University of Oklahoma fans attacked football coach Gary Gibbs in 1992. After the Sooners lost to their traditional archenemy, the University of Texas, fans screamed abuse at Gibbs and covered him with beer.[19]

At some stadiums, visiting coaches practically need to don football helmets to protect their safety. At various times when Dallas coach Jimmy Johnson has played the Eagles in Philadelphia's Veterans Stadium, he's been hit in the head with a battery, beer, and snowballs.[20]

Some sports executives are finally taking strong measures to protect athletes and coaches. As a way of trying to curtail abusive fans, the NBA passed a rule in 1981 that gives teams the right to yank the season tickets of holders who are verbally abusive or whose conduct interferes with a coach's ability to talk to his team during a time-out. Fans are allowed a warning and two ejections before the rule can be invoked.[21]

The first fan to get a warning was Robin Ficker, a forty-eight-year-old attorney from Maryland who has a season ticket to Washington Bullets games. With his booming voice and biting sense of humor, he draws the line at little except profanity. According to *USA Today,* Ficker consistently manages to upset players from his seat directly behind the visiting team's bench, causing many teams to hold their time-outs away from the bench. He's been spat upon by one coach, soaked with Gatorade by the Golden State Warriors, and drawn a thrown basketball and shoe respectively from Michael Jordan and Isiah Thomas.[22]

Several colleges and high schools have also had to get tough with rowdy fans. People found to be drunk at a University of Florida football game, for example, are arrested as well as ejected.[23]

Violent episodes associated with high school athletics are unquestionably on the increase. Several high school coaches have been assaulted by unruly fans and rival players. Matt Griffin, soccer coach at Bixby High School in Oklahoma, was savagely punched by several members of Tulsa's Nathan Hale High School after a game, seriously injuring his facial nerves, one eye socket, his jaw, and one cheekbone. Two students were suspended for their part in the beating. Griffin was the second high school coach from Oklahoma injured following a sporting event; a basketball coach suffered a broken collarbone when assaulted by fans. And a Utah basketball coach at Tabiona High School was slugged by a father who resented his son's lack of playing time.[24]

In a similar 1992 incident involving unruly fans, high school soccer referee David Welch was assaulted by students from J.E.B. Stuart High School in McLean, Virginia. He sustained a deep facial wound and his car was damaged by thrown rocks. Athletes from J.E.B. Stuart High School were disturbed by their fans' response and sent the referee a get-well card. The previous March, rampaging fans at Camden High School in New Jersey began throwing chairs onto the court following a game against arch-rival Trenton High School. The team was punished for its fans' behavior by being disqualified for play-off games.[25]

Without question, the most brutal, dangerous fans in the world are those associated with soccer. At major sporting events around the world, these fans drink and then attack the fans of rival teams.

In 1985, when the Liverpool team traveled to Brussels, Belgium, to play Turin, Italy's Juventus soccer team, drunken British fans charged their rival fans forty-five minutes before the game was to begin. Fans were armed with knives, fence posts, and bottles. In the crushing aftermath, 38 fans—mainly Italians—were killed and 437 were injured. Incredibly, on this Black Wednesday, as it was later called, the two teams made a mockery of the deaths by finishing the game. Officials feared a worse riot might result if they postponed the game.[26]

This was not the only brawl British fans began. In 1972, when the Glasgow Rangers played in Spain, a bloody riot ensued at the Barcelona stadium.[27] In 1988, German and English fans clashed in Dusseldorf, Germany, before and after the European Football (soccer) Championships.[28]

In 1989, some 3,000 Liverpool fans again rioted, many of them upset because they had been unable to obtain tickets for a national cup semifinal match against Nottingham Forest.[29]

Fearful of violence, a policeman opened a gate outside the stadium and thousands of people stormed forward, pushing unsuspecting spectators into a fence intended to keep the Liverpudlians from run-

Victims of a 1985 soccer riot that erupted during a Liverpool-Turin European Soccer Cup Final in Brussels. Thirty-eight people died and several hundred were injured in the incident.

ning onto the field. The result was utter chaos. People were crushed against the fence and suffocated. Before order could be restored, hundreds of fans were injured and ninety-four people, many of them children, died.[30]

The problem, according to *Sports Illustrated* soccer writer Clive Gammon, is that thousands of fans follow their soccer team with no other motivation than to assault opposing fans. Because British soccer stadiums are antiquated and not conducive to crowd control, mass stampedes are inevitable, given the heavy drinking and rowdiness present at games.

Other riots among fans have led to violence and death at stadiums in Barcelona, Bangladesh, and Iraq in 1992, South Africa in 1991, Nigeria in 1989, Mexico City in 1988, Colombia in 1982, Argentina and Turkey in 1968, and Peru in 1964, according to Gammon.

U.S. fans have also been known to riot, although not during a soccer match. Following the Detroit Tigers' victory in the 1984 World Series, Detroit fans went wild outside the stadium, burning cars and hurling rocks at police. One man was killed. A similar riot had occurred in 1979 in Pittsburgh following the Pirates' win over Baltimore in seven games. There were 128 injured, considerable property damage, and an incident in which a woman had been pulled out of her car and threatened with harm.

In professional hockey, after Philadelphia beat the Boston Bruins 1–0 for a championship, fans smashed windows and overturned automobiles—all in the name of celebration. Not infrequently, fans hit hockey players with various objects. When Buffalo Sabres left wing Rob Ray was attacked by a fan in Quebec City, he exacted full revenge by beating the fan.

When fans drink to intoxication at major sport-

One notable instance of fans going out of control was the riot that took place in Detroit after the Tigers won the 1984 World Series.

ing events, the time is ripe for rioting, say sports psychologists. When group behavior takes over, these people are no longer accountable for their actions. "People carry around a lot of built-up frustrations," sports psychologist Bruce Ogilvie of San Jose State has said to the press. "Those feelings of helplessness inevitably bring about rage. . . . [Sports] can be a catalyst. You have an 'enemy,' real or imagined—the visiting fans."

Perhaps the ugliest incident on record was a rematch between Cleveland and the Texas Rangers on June 4, 1974, after the two teams had fought with each other the previous time they played. Many of the hometown Indians' fans had gotten inebriated on discounted ten-cent beer. They first assaulted the visiting team's bull-pen pitchers and catchers with beer cans and firecrackers, forcing them to come into the dugout. In the ninth, they stormed the field, intimidating players in the Texas dugout until home team players pacified the crowd. "If it wasn't for the Cleveland players tonight, we would have got killed," said one Texas player.[31]

One of the ugliest riots in college basketball occurred during a game between Minnesota and the visiting Buckeyes of Ohio State. After Minnesota players kicked and mauled a couple of Ohio State players near the end of the game, mayhem broke out in the stands. The governor of Ohio called the incident "gang warfare in an athletic arena," according to author James Michener.

A similar episode erupted in New York's Felt Forum after fans of boxer Pedro Soto went wild when Mike Quarry outpointed him. The fans destroyed everything they could get their hands on, then set the building on fire. Fans at Roosevelt Raceway in the Long Island section of New York also overreacted after results were allowed to stand, even though six of eight horses had been taken out of the race because of an accident. The fans rampaged, attacked a patrol judge, and overturned cars in the parking lot. The chief of security collapsed with a fatal heart attack.[32]

Even the fans who worship athletes have become a problem. Players have become increasingly impatient with autograph seekers because they say people want them only to sell and because fans often jostle the athletes in the process. It's not unheard of for a fan to thrust fifty or one hundred cards at an athlete, demanding signatures on all of them. In 1991, Cincinnati Reds third baseman Chris Sabo refused to give a fan in St. Louis an autograph following a losing ballgame. When the fan pressed the ballplayer for an explanation, Sabo allegedly shoved him against a plate glass window, shattering the glass. Unhurt, the fan refused to press charges and Reds manager Lou Piniella elected not to discipline Sabo.[33]

Some people actually produce counterfeit signatures of players, selling them to unsuspecting buyers. Baseball cards have become so profitable that some individuals have begun counterfeiting cards to sell to collectors. In April of 1992, the Leaf Sports Trading Cards Company sued Paisano Publications and three of its employees for allegedly counterfeiting copies of Chicago White Sox star Frank Thomas's rookie card. One of the cards, valued at up to seventy dollars was allegedly sold to an off-duty police officer who investigated the matter.[34]

9

SUDDEN DEATH AND SERIOUS INJURIES

In no other sport has the practice of inflicting injury on an opponent become as common as it is in professional hockey. Today, many teams employ so-called goons to stop an opponent's momentum with elbows, fists, and even sticks. A goon is successful if he can get a rival star out of a game through injury or a stay in the penalty box. Others ignore the National Hockey League's goalie interference rule, charging hard into the bodies of rival players to score goals that violate the spirit of fair play.

A violent player appeals to a certain breed of fan, but they've driven away those who prefer clean, legal play. The practice of using goons escalated during the 1986–87 season. Players such as Bob Probert and Joey Kocur of Detroit, Torrie Robertson of Hartford, and Calgary's Tim Hunter won games by roughing up the competition. Fights on the ice began to be premeditated, calculated to upset rival players. In just fifty-three games during the 1986–87 season, Robertson participated in thirty-two fights.

The main targets of a player's aggression are players who are too talented to resort to unsports-

Torrie Robertson of the Hartford Whalers earned a reputation for roughing up the opposition.

manlike tactics. During the 1992 National Hockey League play-offs, a Chicago Blackhawks star suffered torn lips, a bruised cheek, and a scuffed nose caused by St. Louis players. In the same play-offs, a player slashed Pittsburgh star Mario Lemieux, breaking a bone in his left hand.

Some coaches have become fed up with teams that employ violence as a part of their day-to-day strategy. "If that's what this game comes down to—taking the skills away from a guy by pushing his face in—then we're in the wrong business," Edmonton co-coach John Muckler told the press.

Canadian courts have ruled that even life-threatening behavior on the ice should be left to league authorities to punish. In 1969, NHL players Ted Green and Wayne Maki were indicted after slamming each other's skulls with sticks. Green was hit so hard that his skull was fractured and a plate had to be surgically implanted. Neither player went to jail. "Hockey cannot be played without what normally are called assaults," ruled Canadian judge Michael Fitzpatrick. Thus far, U.S. courts have stayed out of professional hockey rinks.[1]

For the first time, during the 1992–93 season, the NHL instituted some strong steps against players who instigate fights, because owners and fans complained about the mauling of their favorite stars. In an attempt to bring finesse back to the sport, those who instigate premeditated fights are being slapped with game misconduct penalties. Nonetheless, the league has yet to get tough on dirty players who get away with violations such as eye gouging during pileups, gratuitous checks on stars outside the center of play, and slashes to the legs with hockey sticks.[2]

Mayhem is often common as well in hydroplane racing, a sport whose heroes are often seriously injured or may even die while competing. One mistake in a career is often fatal for drivers. Two of the greatest hydroplane pilots in history—Bill Muncey and Dean Chenoweth—both died in spectacular, foamy crashes. The greatest hydroplane racer of the 1990s, Chip Hanauer, survived a nasty accident in 1992.

Hydroplane racing tolerates no errors. Three-ton (2.7 t) boats skim the water at speeds in excess of 200 miles (320 km) per hour, upending when a driver overestimates his skill or his craft's capabilities. Drivers are strapped into ticking bombs while other ticking bombs fly past.

Muncey's death was lamented by his many fans; his sixty-two career wins were the most ever in hydroplane racing, making him the Babe Ruth of his sport. He died at age fifty-two, when his boat flipped over backward and landed on top of both him and the surface of the water at the 1981 World Championships in Mexico. He died that evening in a hospital despite attempts by doctors to revive him. His spinal cord had been severed.[3]

According to his widow, Fran Muncey, her husband and other hydroplane drivers had one thing in common: "I've noticed that really good drivers have killer instinct," she says. "They're not afraid of death."[4]

Although baseball is a relatively safe sport, injury and even death are always possibilities when a ball reaching speeds of 93 to 100 miles (149 to 160 km) per hour comes at a batter's head. So it was on August 16, 1920, when Cleveland shortstop Ray Chapman came to bat against Carl Mays of the Giants at New York's Polo Grounds. Chapman was a plate hugger while Mays was a submarine pitcher whose delivery and pitches were hard to follow. He also thought nothing of knocking down a hitter like Chapman.

Mays was using a badly scuffed ball, a not uncommon practice in those days, when owners wanted to save any pennies they could. The count was one and one when there was the crack—similar to the crack of a bat against horsehide—and the ball came to the pitcher. Thinking the ball had hit Chapman's bat, Mays fielded the ball until he saw his catcher, Muddy Ruel, holding the unconscious batter in his arms.

For a brief moment, it looked as if all would be well. Chapman got up and began walking to the clubhouse, but collapsed again. Rushed to a hospital, the player was operated on but failed to survive the operation. He died at dawn the next morning. Mays was interrogated by a New York district attorney. No charges were brought against him, and throughout his long career, he continued to knock batters down as part of his strategy.[5]

Some good did come from Chapman's death. Rules were changed so that umpires threw scuffed balls out of play, balls that can move unpredictably into the path of a batter. Although many people tried to make batting helmets mandatory, players resisted this until the 1950s.[6]

Nonetheless, injuries from blows to the head continue to occur. Many careers have either ended or lost their luster as a result of players being hit in the head. Those major leaguers who were never the same after being hit in the head include Mickey Cochrane, Dickie Thon, Don Zimmer (who had a metal plate in his head as a result), Tony Conigliaro, Paul Blair, and Minnie Minoso. Minor leaguers Johnny Dodge, Jesse Batterson, and Ottis Johnson died as a result of head injuries. Batterson's death devastated Swede Carlson, the pitcher who hit him. He was at the batter's side when he died in 1933.[7]

Because pitchers routinely brush back batters

as a part of everyday strategy, many hitters have begun to retaliate. Fights involving hitters and pitchers are commonplace. These fights often escalate to include the whole team, and players frequently run toward the combatants even from the bull pen to join the fray.

What has troubled many sports authorities is that behavior is tolerated on the field that would place these same players in jail if done off the field. High school and college students who get into fights on the field may be emulating professional athletes.

An incident occurred in 1963 that came close to resulting in the serious injury of Los Angeles catcher John Roseboro. Batter Juan Marichal of San Francisco, believing that the catcher had thrown a ball too close to his head when returning it to the pitcher, repeatedly clubbed Roseboro's head with his bat. Police refused to arrest Marichal, terming it a baseball matter. Although the National League fined and suspended Marichal, many people in the baseball community felt that a stronger punishment was called for. "The act of wielding a bat, rather than the ball, against an opponent was regarded by all as . . . a tactic which . . . couldn't possibly be considered relevant to the strategic and psychological requirements of the game," wrote sportswriter Mike Roberts.[8]

Football is far more dangerous than baseball. In the beginning days of college football, the game depended on bruising, senseless formations like the so-called flying wedge in which the whole team came at defenders. By 1905, deaths on the college football field had become frighteningly commonplace: eighteen players had died and 159 serious injuries had occurred.

The NCAA was formed to enact reforms but detractors thought the attempt was futile. "It is childish to suppose that the athletic authorities who have permitted football to become such a brutal ... game could be trusted to reform it," said then-Harvard president Charles Eliot. The game came close to extinction when President Theodore Roosevelt warned universities that if rules changes were not enacted to make football less dangerous, it would have to be outlawed. The next year, the Intercollegiate Football Association tried to clean up the game by expelling anyone for "fighting or kneeing an opposing player." By 1910, so-called flying tackles were also disallowed.[9]

Nonetheless, players continue to be injured. In recent years, several players in the NFL have been paralyzed, including Darryl Stingley, Dennis Byrd, and Mike Utley. The death of college player Roy Lee (Chucky) Mullins of the University of Mississippi is a tragic example for the 1990s of how death can be only one tackle away. On May 1, 1991, as Mullins got ready for class, he collapsed with a blood clot in his lungs. Rushed to a hospital in nearby Memphis, Tennessee, he lived for five days.

Mullins had been injured during the 1989 season in Ole Miss's Homecoming Game against Vanderbilt. He had raced over from his free safety position to tackle wide receiver Brad Gaines, who had caught a pass from his quarterback. Despite the crowd noise, everyone heard the impact of the two bodies colliding, accompanied by an ominous "crack" that frightened everyone on the field. Mullins had sustained a broken neck and shattered spine, rendering him a quadriplegic.[10]

More scandalous than the occasional football death are the continued serious injuries and deaths that occur during boxing matches. Several deaths have caused doctors and sports figures such as Howard Cosell, a onetime boxing commentator, to call for a ban on the sport. Jess Willard killed Bull Young with a right hook to the jaw in 1913. In 1927, middleweight champion Tiger Flowers died four days after winning a bout with heavyweight boxer Leo Gates at Madison Square Garden.[11] In 1937, bantamweight Tony Marino of Pittsburgh died following an eight-round beating at the hands of Indian Quintana.

The 1962 death of Benny "Kid" Paret, at that time the twentieth fighter to die in the ring, was particularly lurid. Because referee Ruby Goldstein failed to halt the match while the boxer was immobilized in the ropes, boxer Emile Griffith kept slugging away at the victim's head. Griffith was incensed because his opponent had insulted him during the weigh-in. Paret, who defeated Don Jordan for the welterweight crown in 1960, was rushed to a hospital but died ten days after the fight. Blood clots had filled his brain, and he died in a coma, having never regained consciousness.[12]

The next year, 1963, Davey Moore died of a brain hemorrhage in his dressing room following a featherweight bout with Sugar Ramos. Sportswriter Jim Murray quoted a ringsider as saying the match was a game of "Russian roulette with six-ounce gloves."[13]

More recently, Duk Koo Kim of Korea died in 1982 following a bout with Ray "Boom-Boom" Mancini in the lightweight division. Another tragedy and near fatality occurred in 1991, when twenty-two-year-old Kid Akeem Anifowoshe went into a coma after taking more than 400 blows to the head in a single bantamweight match with champion Robert Quiroga. Anifowoshe lived, but was paralyzed.[14] In addition, the tragic disintegration of Muhammad Ali's health, thought by many experts to be a direct result of too many blows to the head, has

Ray "Boom-Boom" Mancini successfully defends his lightweight boxing title against Duk Koo Kim of Korea in 1982 in a bout that proved fatal for Kim.

inspired many people to ask that boxing be outlawed.

"The man who took punches for twenty-seven years, twenty-one as a pro, is punch-drunk and brain damaged," says his friend, longtime sports announcer Howard Cosell. When Ali was well past his prime, he took a terrible beating from boxer Larry Holmes, a bout that should have been stopped before it began. The only reason Ali was not killed in the ring is because Holmes pulled many punches to try to protect his boyhood idol, said Cosell.[15]

Like boxing deaths, auto racing deaths have become frighteningly common. In 1987, the man who was called the "Grand Old Man" of racing, Jim Fitzgerald, died at the age of sixty-five when his Nissan 300ZX Turbo slammed into a concrete wall during the GTE St. Petersburg Grand Prix. The death attracted national attention and discussion on whether there needed to be a mandatory retirement age for racers. Fitzgerald's longtime partner, who was in that last fatal race with him, was then-sixty-two-year-old Paul Newman, the actor and driver.[16]

Before his last race, Fitzgerald had complained that people his age gave him no respect. "You'd think people my age would get excited about it, but they don't," he told the *Tampa Tribune*. "They tell me I'm crazy."[17]

Severe injuries and death in racing are "the nature of the business, this cruelest of sports," writes sportswriter Bill Libby. One of the first to die in a major race, Bob Burman, a record-setting driver, was killed in 1916 with his mechanic when a tire on his Peugeot blew out and his car slammed into two telephone poles. Ironically, he had once told a writer that he expected to crash someday and to die in his wife's arms. He did just that.[18]

In 1928, a promising twenty-five-year-old

Car driven by Philippe Gache of France collides in the 1992 Indy 500. Auto racing is perhaps the deadliest of sports.

driver, Frank Lockhart, went all out to try to break the land-speed record at Daytona Beach. He would have done it, too, but at 225 miles (360 km) per hour, he drove over a seashell and a tire exploded. He was thrown from the car and landed at his wife's feet.[19]

One of the most famous drivers of all time, Jimmy Murphy, was so well known that in the 1920s a popular foxtrot was named after him. He died at the age of thirty in 1924 at a New York State dirt track when he hit a fence, driving a piece of wood into his heart.[20]

The list of fatalities in auto racing goes on and on. In the 1933 Indianapolis 500 alone, three drivers and two mechanics were killed. In 1948, an outstanding driver, Ted Horn, was superstitious about the color green and refused to let either women or children near him before a race. He died in a race at Du Quoin, Illinois, after he had reluctantly let his wife and children attend the race. His wife had been wearing a green outfit.[21]

In 1949, racing legend Rex Mays died in a race at Del Mar, California, when he was flung out of his car. He had always had an aversion to seat belts and refused to wear them. Had he worn one he might have suffered only minor injuries.[22]

In 1955, two-time Indy-winning driver Bill "Mad Russian" Vukovich felt that he should pull out of the Indy 500 event and told his wife so. But he went on as planned. In the lead after 125 miles (200 km), there was a pileup and Vukovich's racing car bounced like a toy, crashed, and burned. He died of a broken skull. The man who won the race died about a year later while driving in another race.[23]

In 1961, test-driving a friend's car at Indy, veteran driver Tony Bettenhausen was killed when he slammed the car into a wall. He had once blasted critics of the sport. "A lot of years can go by without a single fatal accident in a given race, then let one driver get killed in one race and people start talking about abolishing the sport," he complained. "It's not fair."[24]

In August 1992, Clifford Allison, the son of famed auto racer Bobby Allison, died at Michigan International Raceway during a practice run. A tire blew out, catapulting the vehicle into a wall a few days before the start of a Grand National race. The twenty-seven-year-old Allison was a novice in the sport and had not yet won a motor sports race. Three weeks before Clifford's death, his brother Davey Allison had broken a collarbone, arm, and wrist in a near-fatal collision during an auto race in Long Pond, Pennsylvania.[25] (Davey Allison subsequently died in a helicopter crash.)

By 1992, many critics were saying that racing had become too dangerous and that something had to be done to make the sport safer. At the Indy 500, for example, the presence of the concrete wall and cars that routinely traveled 220 miles (352 km) per hour and better had critics demanding that the sport be made safer. The 1992 Indy race was as crash-filled as any on record. In addition to the death of one driver in a preliminary bout, the Memorial Day race itself was a horror. Unseasonably cold temperatures assailed the track, making it nearly impossible for tires to properly grip the track. Mario Andretti, fifty-two, and his twenty-eight-year-old son, Jeff, crashed; the younger Andretti was seriously injured, fracturing his feet and ankles and sustaining a concussion. All told, thirteen drivers were involved in ten pileups.[26]

A national scandal sometimes occurs when an athlete snaps in the middle of a competition. During the late 1970s, basketball star Kermit Washington of Los Angeles lost his temper after a shoving match with Houston's Rudy Tomjanovich. He took a running swing at Tomjanovich and shattered the Rocket's jaw, ending Tomjanovich's career. Tomjanovich sued Los Angeles management and won a multimillion-dollar decision in 1979.

Many athletes feel intense pressure to perform and feel that they've let everyone down if they fail.

Just how intense that pressure really can be became shockingly clear in 1986.

A junior from North Carolina State, Kathy Love Ormsby was a classic overachiever—the 1983 valedictorian of her high school class, holder of multiple state running records, and top premed student. Having recently broken the U.S. collegiate record for 10,000 meters, Ormsby was entered in that same event during the NCAA championships. A little more than halfway through the race she was trailing in fourth place when she decided to make her move. Instead of trying to pass the trio of women ahead, Ormsby bolted from the track and began racing down an Indianapolis avenue. Confused, her parents, who were in attendance, asked Indiana University security officers to look for her.[27]

The first person to find the runner was her coach, Rollie Geiger. Ormsby had decided during the race to end her life. She leaped over the railing of a bridge, landing on the banks of the White River. She had multiple injuries, including a fractured vertebra, which would paralyze her from the waist down for the rest of her life. "She could easily have died," said one of her neurosurgeons.[28]

Ormsby was just one of many athletes who have been unable to cope with the pressures of big-time athletics combined with the grueling demands of college studies. "If she didn't come in first she had a tendency to think that she was letting a lot of other people down," said Charlie Bishop, her high school track coach. "Winning was not just for herself. I don't think this was something on the spur of the moment that said, 'Kathy, get off the track.' I think it was something that had been building for a period of time."[29]

Driven to win, other athletes have taken their

own lives. Athletes are not immune from the demons that haunt other people. In baseball, as of 1992, at least ninety-seven professional baseball players, managers, and executives had committed suicide.[30] One of the most haunting deaths in the history of sports was the death of twenty-nine-year-old Willard Hershberger, a catcher for the Cincinnati Reds, on August 3, 1940. A fine hitter, he had batted .345 in a part-time role the previous year.

Hershberger's Reds, in first place in the National League by six games, were playing a doubleheader against the Bees in Boston. But the catcher was listening to the game on his portable radio in his hotel room instead of warming up at the park. The game was the last thing he heard. Hershberger committed suicide sometime around the seventh inning, the only baseball player to commit suicide during a season, according to *Sports Illustrated.*[31]

The death of one of the country's most beloved athletes, Flo Hyman, shocked followers of the sport in 1986. Called "the best American woman volleyball player ever" by *Sports Illustrated,* the death of the dynamic star of the 1984 Olympics was due to the rupturing of an enlarged and "dime-sized weak spot in her aorta," according to that publication.[32]

Hyman's last minutes occurred while she was playing in a Japanese volleyball league. She sat down on the bench following a substitution, and died instantly at the age of thirty-one.[33] She died of a condition known as Marfan's syndrome, and her death raised the national consciousness about the disease. Hyman's death caused many doctors to call for the testing of tall people with a somewhat gaunt look, indented breastbones, inordinately long fingers and toes, and nearsightedness, all symptoms of the disease Hyman died of. Interestingly, some experts have argued that Abraham Lincoln might have had the syndrome, which is caused by defective genes.[34]

Significantly, although prior to Hyman's death few in the sports world were aware of Marfan's, the disease had made itself known previously. A University of Maryland basketball player, 6-foot nine-inch (2-m) Chris Patton, had died while dunking a ball in a pickup game on campus.[35]

Another death that particularly affected Americans who had taken up exercising late in life was that of running and fitness guru Jim Fixx. His 1984 death while running in northern Vermont intrigued and frightened the many fans of the man whose book, *The Complete Book of Running,* had fueled the fitness craze during the late 1970s and early 1980s. Because of Fixx, many Americans had taken up running to improve their own health.

The reason he was so successful, said *The Runner,* was because he was the epitome of the unhealthy American who decides to redeem himself. In 1967, this heavy-smoking, overweight, stressed-out magazine executive vowed to turn his life around. He threw out his cigarettes, watched his diet, and began competing in marathons. Then he wrote a book on running that was a runaway best-seller, selling about 1 million copies.[36]

Why did he die? For one reason, he had a near phobia about doctors, rarely getting checkups and never getting a stress test. This was unfortunate, because an autopsy showed that he had already suffered some minor heart damage. In 1980, during one of his infrequent checkups, his total cholesterol count was much higher than the average person's. Genetics contributed, and the stress from an acrimonious divorce hadn't helped his health. Simply put, although running had lessened his risk of death from

*Jim Fixx popularized the sport
of running through his best-selling*
The Complete Book of Running.
He died during a run in 1984.

a heart attack, it had not eliminated it. The autopsy showed tremendous blockage in his arteries; one had been 95 percent blocked. Fixx's death taught Americans a lesson that not enough people pay attention to. It isn't enough to exercise. A runner must also consult medical practitioners to fight pre-existing disease and to monitor changing health conditions.[37]

An athlete is sometimes diagnosed with a serious condition but tries to defy the odds, often with dire consequences. In 1990, six-seven (2-m) center-forward Hank Gathers of Loyola Marymount University jammed home a stunning dunk against Portland State. But while cheers rang in his ears, he dropped to the floor, writhing in convulsions. A doctor, team trainer, and his mother ran onto the court in a futile effort to assist him. The twenty-three-year-old Gathers was dead.

Gathers had known he had a serious heart problem since the previous December. He had collapsed during another college game, and tests showed that he had an irregular heartbeat. Heavily medicated, he returned to action quickly, missing only two games. But because the medication slowed him down, he reduced his doses to almost nothing and played well enough to become a likely first-round NBA draft pick. A poor kid from the wrong side of Philadelphia, he strove for excellence on every play. "Hank was an incredible life force, a walking thunderbolt," said his coach, Paul Westhead.[38]

In the months after the funeral, Gathers's mother argued that the team doctors should not have allowed her son to reduce his medication. In March 1992, Loyola Marymount agreed to pay Mrs. Gathers $545,000 to settle her wrongful-death lawsuit.[39]

Because deaths like these of supposedly healthy athletes are so unexpected, fans are traumatized whenever a player dies in action. Thus far no ath-

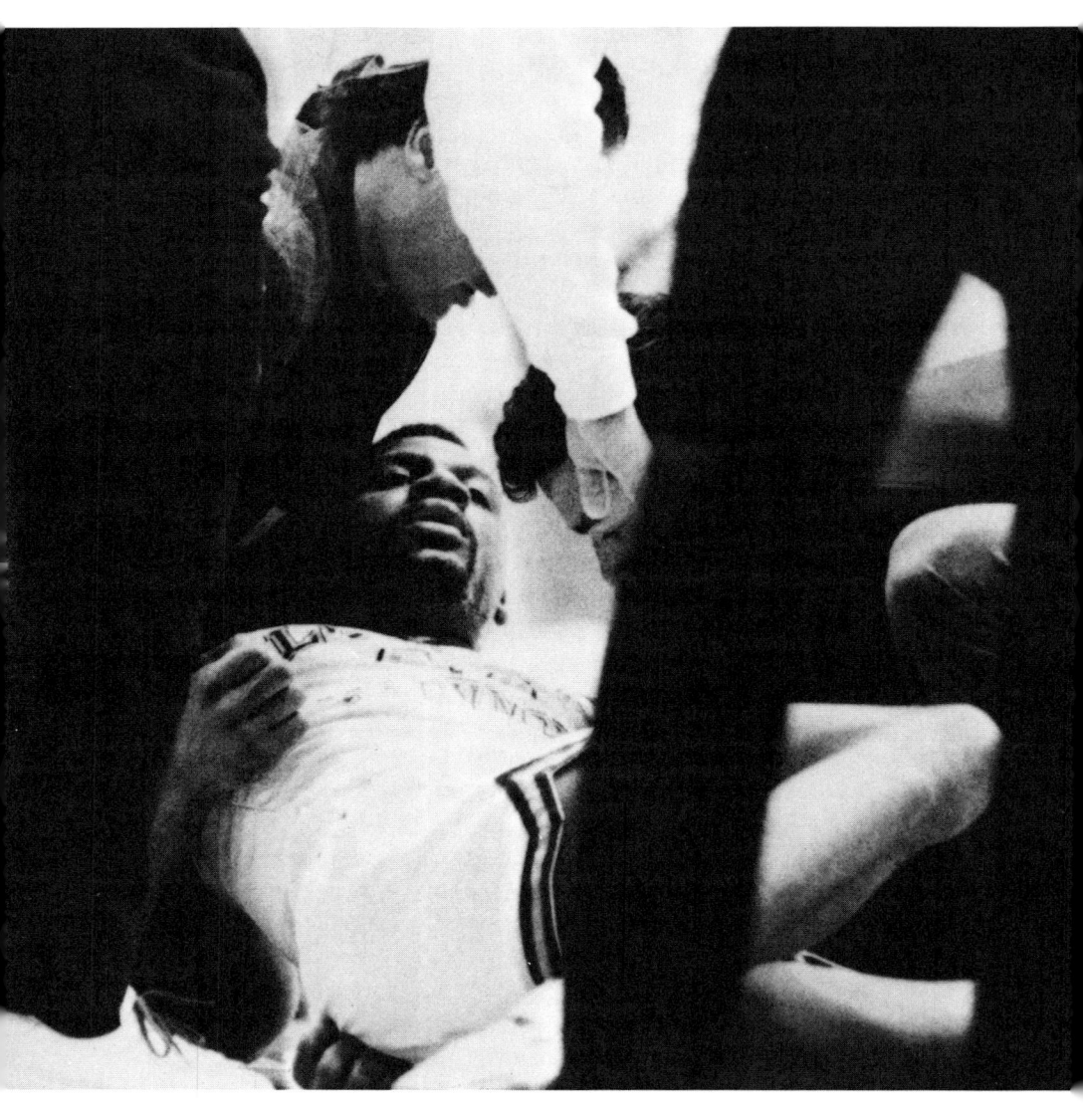

Loyola-Marymount basketball star Hank Gathers died during a West Coast Conference Tournament in 1990.

letes have been murdered on the playing field, but in 1978, California Angels hitting star Lyman Bostock was killed hours after going two for four at the plate against the Chicago White Sox. He had the misfortune of riding in the same car with a woman whose estranged husband went after her with a shotgun. Perhaps thinking that Bostock was having an affair with his wife (the player wasn't), the husband fired into the car, killing the athlete and wounding his wife. The news sickened baseball for days after Bostock's death. He had been one of the most talented hitters and best-liked men in the game.[40]

On one occasion the deaths of athletes became an international incident. In 1972, during the Munich Olympics, Arab terrorists slaughtered Israeli athletes. The German people, mindful of how the world viewed Hitler's destruction of the Jews during World War II, were aghast that this tragedy occurred on their soil. An estimated 900 million people watched events transpire on television.[41]

Arab terrorists entered the Olympic Village in the dark, early-morning hours of September 5, easily scaling a fence that surrounded the complex. Three terrorists had gotten credentials to work in the complex, and they had a fair knowledge of where their quarry would be. They carried weapons in canvas sacks. They removed the athletic clothing of competing nations that they wore and donned masks and disguises. Then they marched into the building that held members of the Israeli Olympic team and delegation. They killed two Israelis and took nine hostage. When German police attacked the terrorists at the airport, the Arabs massacred the hostages. Three terrorists survived the police assault and were taken into custody. Israel retaliated with raids on Lebanon and Syria, and the slayings in part led to war between Arabs and Israel in 1973.[42]

The story of the 1994 Olympics that drew the most press coverage was a scandal that occurred right before the final qualification trials for the ice-skating event. In a scene horrifyingly reminiscent of the attack on tennis pro Monica Selles, world-champion skater Nancy Kerrigan was assaulted on January 6, 1994. One of her legs was severely bruised when her assailant whacked her outside a Detroit rink. She was there to compete in the U.S. National Championships, a competition won by Tonya Harding; the assault on Kerrigan prevented her from skating.

Equally shocking were the arrests that occurred several days after the incident. Investigators charged four men with conspiracy in a plot to take Kerrigan out of the Olympics—a plot that failed when Kerrigan was named to the team anyway. Two of the four were men close to skating competitor Tonya Harding. One was her former husband; the other was Harding's bodyguard. They implicated Harding in the event, saying that she had full knowledge that it was going to occur.

Harding, while denying that she was a part of the plot, told reporters that she had failed to cooperate with investigators citing "shock and fear" for her own safety. Harding pleaded with the U.S. Olympic Committee, asking its members not to ban her from competition. In a statement to the press she said, "I ask only for your understanding and the opportunity to represent my country with the best figure-skating performance of my life."

On January 31, 1994, the last day for the committee to submit a roster of skaters for the 1994 Winter Olympics, even while the investigation continued, Harding was among those chosen.

SOURCE NOTES

CHAPTER ONE

1. *The Sporting News,* Special Issue: "The Year in Sports (1990)," pp. 16–17. See also Jill Lieber and Craig Neff, *Sports Illustrated* (July 3, 1989), pp. 10–25.
2. Howard Cosell, *What's Wrong with Sports* (New York: Pocket Books, 1991), p. 22.
3. *USA Today,* August 14, 1991, p. 5C.
4. *USA Today,* January 9, 1992, p. 5C.
5. Donald Honig, *The Greatest First Basemen of All Time* (New York: Crown, 1988), p. 10.
6. Ibid., p. 10.
7. Harold Seymour, *Baseball: The Golden Age* (New York: Oxford University Press, 1971), pp. 278–79.
8. Ibid., p. 300.
9. Ibid., p. 303.
10. *USA Today,* June 25, 1991, p. 9C.
11. *USA Today,* June 25, 1991, p. 9C. See also David Harris, *The League* (New York: Bantam, 1986), p. 45.

12. Cosell, p. 145. See also Armen Keteyian, "The Straight-Arrow Addict," *Sports Illustrated* (March 10, 1986), pp. 74–77, and *USA Today,* July 21, 1992, p. 1C.

13. Robert Sullivan, "Gambling, Payoffs and Drugs," *Sports Illustrated* (October 30, 1989), pp. 40–45.

14. *USA Today,* October 14, 1992, 13C.

15. Russell Rice *Big Blue Machine* (Tomball, Texas: Strode Publishers, 1988), pp. 217, 227.

16. Philip Straw, "Point Spreads and Journalistic Ethics," in Richard E. Lapchick, ed., *Fractured Focus: Sport as a Reflection of Society* (Lexington, Massachusetts: Lexington Books, 1986), p. 263.

17. Hank Nuwer, "Under the Volcano," *Sport* (February 1989), pp. 50–56.

18. Jim Savage, *The Encyclopedia of the NCAA Basketball Tournament* (New York: Dell, 1990), p. 75.

19. Nuwer, "Volcano," pp. 50–56.

20. Geoffrey Norman, "After the Fall," *Sports Illustrated* (May 20, 1991), pp. 72–88.

21. Savage, p. 201.

22. Straw, p. 265.

23. *The Chronicle of Higher Education,* June 12, 1991, p. A30. See also *USA Today,* July 23, 1992, p. 11C, and October 20, 1992, p. 15C.

24. Norman, p. 76.

25. Ibid.

26. *The Sporting News,* March 30, 1992, p. 5.

27. *USA Today,* April 2, 1992, p. 2C.

28. *The Sporting News,* March 30, 1992, p. 5.

29. Ibid.

30. H. Roy Kaplan, "Sports Gambling and Television: The Emerging Alliance," in Lapchick, pp. 253–254. See also Cosell, p. 155.

31. Ibid.

32. Ibid., p. 254.
33. Ibid., p. 245; pp. 254–55. See also *USA Today,* June 27, 1991, 1C.
34. *The Sporting News,* March 25, 1991, p. 6. See also *USA Today,* June 25, 1991, p. 9C.
35. Sullivan, "Gambling," p. 40.

CHAPTER TWO

1. Edward S. Jordan, "Buying Football Victories," *Collier's* (November 25, 1905), pp. 21–24.
2. Ibid.
3. Ibid.
4. Ibid.
5. See "1985: A Year of Crisis in College Athletics," *Lexington Herald-Leader* (NCAA reprint), 1986, pp. 1–16.
6. Ibid.
7. Nuwer, "Under the Volcano," p. 53.
8. Ibid.
9. See "A Year of Crisis," 10–16.
10. Robert Sullivan and Craig Neff, "Shame on You, SMU," *Sports Illustrated* (March 9, 1987), pp. 18–23.
11. William F. Reed, "The End May Be Nigh," *Sports Illustrated* (November 11, 1991), pp. 84–89. See also *USA Today,* October 21, 1991, p. 12C, and Ian Thomsen, "His Father's Burden," *The National* (January 30, 1991), pp. 30–33.
12. Kaplan, p. 245.
13. Thomsen, p. 32.
14. *The Chronicle of Higher Education,* April 29, 1992, p. A31.
15. Robert Sullivan, "Time to Play [Tad] Foote Ball," *Sports Illustrated* (December 21, 1987), 58–63.
16. Ibid., p. 60.

17. Phil Taylor, "New Day Dawns in Arkansas," *Sports Illustrated* (January 13, 1992), 39–40.

18. Sullivan, "Foote Ball," p. 60.

19. Nuwer, "Volcano," p. 52. See also Alexander Wolff and Armen Keteyian, *Raw Recruits* (New York: Pocket Books, 1991), p. 168.

20. Wolff and Keteyian, pp. 167–68.

21. *USA Today,* June 17, 1991, p. 2A.

22. Austin Murphy, "Goodbye Columbus," *Sports Illustrated* (September 9, 1991), pp. 46–49.

23. William Nack, "This Case Was One for the Books," *Sports Illustrated* (February 24, 1986), pp. 34–42.

24. Ibid.

25. *USA Today,* June 20, 1991, p. 2C.

26. *The Sporting News,* August 31, 1992, p. 47.

27. Ibid.

28. *USA Today,* April 24, 1992, pp. 1C, 12C.

29. William F. Reed, "What Price Glory?" *Sports Illustrated* (December 24, 1990), pp. 34–38.

30. E. M. Swift, "The Graduates," *Sports Illustrated* (June 8, 1987), pp. 60–64.

CHAPTER THREE

1. *USA Today,* May 15, 1992, p. 2C.

2. Lyle Alzado with Shelley Smith, "I'm Sick and I'm Scared," *Sports Illustrated* (July 8, 1991), pp. 21–27.

3. Smith, Shelley, "A Doctor's Warning Ignored," *Sports Illustrated* (July 8, 1991), pp. 22–23.

4. *USA Today,* August 13, 1991, p. 10C.

5. Peter King, "We Can Clean It Up," *Sports Illustrated* (July 9, 1990), pp. 34–38.

6. *USA Today,* July 26, 1991, p. 1C.

7. *USA Today,* October 8, 1991, p. 3C.

8. *USA Today,* July 10, 1991, p. 11C.

9. Sullivan, "Foote Ball," p. 58.

10. Tommy Chaikin with Rick Telander, "The Nightmare of Steroids," *Sports Illustrated* (October 24, 1988), pp. 82–102.

11. Ibid.

12. Ibid., pp. 89–92.

13. Ibid., p. 97.

14. Ibid., pp. 99–102.

15. *USA Today,* June 20, 1991, p. 1A.

16. *USA Today,* March 25, 1992, p. 2C.

17. *USA Today,* July 1, 1991, p. 9C.

18. *The Sporting News,* January 21, 1991, p. 40.

19. Kenny Moore, "Clean and Slower," *Sports Illustrated* (July 22, 1991), pp. 26–29.

20. Ibid.

21. *USA Today,* October 22, 1991, p. 1C.

22. Bjarne Rostaing and Robert Sullivan, "Triumphs Tainted with Blood," *Sports Illustrated* (January 21, 1985), pp. 12–17. See also *USA Today,* June 20, 1989, 1C.

23. Rostaing, pp. 12–17.

24. *USA Today,* March 10, 1992, p. 9C.

25. Rick Telander and Merrell Noden, "The Death of an Athlete," *Sports Illustrated* (February 20, 1989), pp. 68–78.

26. *USA Today,* August 29, 1991, p. 1C.

CHAPTER FOUR

1. *USA Today,* June 19, 1991, p. 7A.

2. *USA Today,* July 23, 1991, p. 3C.

3. Edward Linn, "The Sad End of Big Daddy," in Irving T. Marsh and Edward Ehre, eds., *Thirty Years of Best Sports Stories* (New York: Dutton, 1975), pp. 188–90.

4. Ibid., pp. 188–89.

5. Rick Telander, "Life Issues from a Man of Steel," *Sports Illustrated* (August 19, 1991), pp. 48–51.

6. *The Sporting News,* January 21, 1991, p. 41.

7. Ibid.

8. Joseph M. Overfield, "Tragedies and Shortened Careers," in John Thorn and Pete Palmer, *Total Baseball* (New York: Warner, 1989), pp. 442–53.

9. Gutman, p. 108.

10. Donald Hall with Dock Ellis, *In the Country of Baseball* (New York: Fireside, 1976, 1989), p. 316.

11. Gary McClain, "A Bad Trip," *Sports Illustrated* (March 16, 1987), cover page +.

12. *USA Today,* October 17, 1991, p. 1C.

13. Thomas Henderson and Peter Knobler, *Out of Control* (New York: G. P. Putnam's Sons, 1987), pp. 12–14.

14. Ibid., p. 12.

15. Ibid., pp. 16, 25.

16. Zimmerman, Paul, "LT on LT," *Sports Illustrated* (September 16, 1991), pp. 40–48.

17. *USA Today,* March 10, 1992, p. 9C.

18. *USA Today,* July 11, 1991, p. 9C.

19. *The Sporting News,* February 18, 1991, 19–20.

20. Ibid.

21. *USA Today,* November 1, 1991, p. 13C.

22. *The Sporting News,* May 20, 1991, p. 12.

23. Ibid., pp. 12–13.

24. *The Sporting News,* January 8, 1990, p. 44.

25. *The Sporting News,* April 9, 1990, p. 34.

26. *The Sporting News,* August 6, 1990, p. 33.

27. Ron Fimrite, "One Pitch at a Time," *Sports Illustrated* (September 17, 1990), pp. 58–63.

28. Jack McCallum, "The Perils of Life in the

Fast Lane," *Sports Illustrated* (July 15, 1985), pp. 36–41.

29. Henderson, p. 7.

CHAPTER FIVE

1. Jules Tygiel, *Baseball's Great Experiment* (New York: Oxford University Press, 1987), pp. 5–6.

2. Leigh Montville, "Beantown: One Tough Place to Play," *Sports Illustrated* (August 19, 1991), p. 46.

3. Ibid.

4. Ibid., pp. 41–43.

5. Ibid., pp. 46–47.

6. Tygiel, pp. 181–84.

7. Ibid., p. 185.

8. *USA Today,* August 13, 1991, p. 4C.

9. Hank Aaron, *If I Had a Hammer* (New York: HarperCollins, 1991), pp. 232–34.

10. Ibid., pp. 230–31.

11. Reggie Jackson, "We Have a Serious Problem," *Sports Illustrated* (May 11, 1987), pp. 40–48.

12. Ibid., p. 47.

13. *The Sporting News,* August 5, 1991, p. 5.

14. *USA Today,* November 5, 1991, 2C.

15. Ibid.

16. Thomsen, pp. 30–33.

17. *USA Today,* December 20, 1991, p. 1C.

18. Thomsen, p. 33.

19. Curry Kirkpatrick, "The Night They Drove Old Dixie Down," *Sports Illustrated* (April 1, 1991), pp. 70–83.

20. Ibid., p. 74.

21. *USA Today,* October 21, 1991, p. 12C.

22. William Oscar Johnson, "It Is Time, It Is Time," *Sports Illustrated* (April 29, 1991), p. 38.

23. *USA Today,* July 9, 1991, 1C.
24. Kenny Moore, "A Courageous Stand," *Sports Illustrated* (August 5, 1991), pp. 62–79.
25. Kenny Moore, "The Eye of the Storm," *Sports Illustrated* (August 12, 1991), pp. 60–73.
26. Richard Demak, "Off Course," *Sports Illustrated* (April 29, 1991), p. 15.
27. Hank Hersch, "Choosing Sides," *Sports Illustrated* (November 27, 1989), pp. 42–63.
28. Ibid., p. 42.
29. *USA Today,* December 17, 1991, p. 2C.
30. Ibid.
31. Ibid.
32. Cosell, pp. 91–92.
33. Bruce Newman, "Black, White—and Gray," *Sports Illustrated* (May 2, 1988), p. 69.
34. *USA Today,* July 11, 1991, p. 6C.

CHAPTER SIX

1. William Nack, "A Gruesome Account," *Sports Illustrated* (February 10, 1992), pp. 24–27.
2. *USA Today,* July 31, 1991, p. 1C.
3. Nack, "Gruesome Account," p. 27.
4. William Nack, "A Crushing Verdict," *Sports Illustrated* (February 17, 1992), pp. 22–23.
5. *USA Today,* February 21, 1992, p. 1C.
6. *USA Today,* August 27, 1991, pp. 2C, 8C.
7. *USA Today,* December 12, 1991, p. 11C.
8. *USA Today,* September 9, 1992, 8C.
9. *USA Today,* August 27, 1991, p. 8C.
10. Ibid.
11. Ibid.
12. Ibid.
13. Ibid.
14. Ibid.
15. Rick Telander and Robert Sullivan, "You

Reap What You Sow," *Sports Illustrated* (February 27, 1989), pp. 20–31.

16. *USA Today,* August 27, 1991, p. 8C.

17. Jerry Kirshenbaum, "An American Disgrace," *Sports Illustrated* (February 27, 1989), pp. 16–19.

18. Leigh Montville, "Season of Torment," *Sports Illustrated* (May 13, 1991), pp. 60–65.

19. *USA Today,* July 17, 1991, p. 8C.

20. *USA Today,* August 3, 1992, 11C.

21. *USA Today,* April 24, 1992, p. 1C.

22. *USA Today,* November 8, 1991, pp. 1–2C.

23. Ibid.

24. *USA Today,* November 12, 1991, p. 6C.

25. E. M. Swift, "Dangerous Games," *Sports Illustrated* (November 10, 1991), pp. 40–41.

26. E. M. Swift, "Facing the Music," *Sports Illustrated* (March 6, 1989), pp. 38–45.

27. *USA Today,* August 13, 1991, p. 1C.

28. Dan Gutman, *Baseball Babylon* (New York: Penguin, 1992), pp. 20–23.

29. Ibid., p. 5. See also Robert W. Creamer, *The Babe* (New York: Penguin, 1974), pp. 320–21.

30. Gutman, pp. 11–13.

31. Ibid., pp. 17–19.

32. *USA Today,* September 18, 1991, 1C.

33. Ibid.

34. Ibid.

35. *The Chronicle of Higher Education,* June 26, 1991, p. A25.

36. Michael Roberts, *Fans* (Washington: The New Republic Book Company, 1976), p. 129.

37. Taylor, "Day," pp. 39–40.

38. Ibid.

39. Ibid.

40. *The Sporting News,* April 20, 1992, p. 6.

41. Al Stump, "Baseball's Biggest Headache,"

in Irving Marsh and Edward Ehre, eds., *Best Sports Stories 1960* (New York: Dutton, 1960), pp. 65–78.

42. Overfield, p. 445.
43. Ibid., pp. 445–46.
44. Cosell, p. 55.
45. Ibid.
46. *USA Today,* September 29, 1992, 13C.

CHAPTER SEVEN

1. *The Sporting News,* September 28, 1992, p. 3.
2. Kaplan, p. 251.
3. *SABR Bulletin,* June 1992, p. 1+.
4. Richard Whittingham, *Saturday Afternoon* (New York: Workman, 1985), p. 77.
5. Ibid.
6. Rick Telander and Robert Sullivan, "You Reap What You Sow," *Sports Illustrated* (February 27, 1989), p. 26.
7. Arch Ward, ed., *The Greatest Sport Stories from the Chicago Tribune* (New York: Barnes, 1953), p. 73.
8. John D. McCallum, *The Encyclopedia of World Boxing Champions* (Radnor, Pennsylvania: Chilton, 1975), p. 170.
9. William Nack, "O Unlucky Man," *Sports Illustrated* (February 4, 1991), pp. 66–80.
10. Joyce Carol Oates, "On Boxing," in Elizabeth Hardwick, ed., *The Best American Essays 1986* (New York: Ticknor & Fields 1986), p. 210.
11. Peter Gammons, "O.K. Drop That Emery Board," *Sports Illustrated* (August 17, 1987), pp. 34–36. See also Thomas Boswell, *How Life Imitates the World Series* (New York: Penguin, 1982), p. 198.
12. Ibid., p. 35.
13. Boswell, p. 200.

14. Gammons, p. 36.
15. Ibid., pp. 34–36.
16. Charles B. Cleveland, *The Great Baseball Managers* (New York: Thomas Y. Crowell Company, 1950), p. 29.
17. Robert Sullivan, "It's Doubles or Nothing," *Sports Illustrated* (August 10, 1987), pp. 60–64.
18. Curry Kirkpatrick, "Signs of the Times," *Sports Illustrated* (September 12, 1988), pp. 54–58.
19. Ibid.
20. *Newsweek,* May 5, 1980, p. 98.
21. Ibid.
22. Hank Nuwer, "A High Wind to Australia," *Satellite Orbit* (October 1986), pp. 39–42.
23. Ibid.
24. *Washington Post,* January 19, 1992, p. D4.
25. *The New York Times,* September 20, 1992, Section 8, p. 1.
26. *The Sporting News,* May 11, 1992, p. 49.
27. Tim Wendel, "Sports and Agents: Illegal Procedure," *Syracuse University Magazine* (March 1990), pp. 34–37. See also *USA Today,* June 20, 1989, 1C.
28. Wendel, p. 34.
29. Ibid., p. 36.
30. Ibid., pp. 36–37.
31. Ibid., p. 35.
32. Ibid., pp. 35, 38.
33. *USA Today,* December 5, 1991, 3C.

CHAPTER EIGHT

1. Stump, pp. 65–78.
2. Gutman, pp. 27–29.
3. Ibid.
4. Ibid.
5. Associated Press, June 2, 1992.

6. Paul D. Adomites, "The Fans," in Thorn, p. 666.
7. Ibid., pp. 666–67.
8. Gutman, pp. 291–92.
9. Creamer, *Babe,* p. 259.
10. Associated Press, December 1, 1990.
11. *USA Today,* November 22, 1991, 1C.
12. Nicholas Dawidoff, "You (Bleep)!" *Sports Illustrated* (June 3, 1991), pp. 50–55.
13. Ibid., p. 54.
14. Ibid.
15. *USA Today,* June 5, 1992, p. 2C.
16. Stan Hochman, "The Day of the Jackals," *Best Sports Stories 1974* (New York: Dutton, 1974), pp. 271–73.
17. Ibid.
18. *USA Baseball Weekly,* June 10–16, 1992, p. 5.
19. *USA Today,* October 21, 1992, p. 1C.
20. *USA Today,* October 1, 1992, 12C.
21. *USA Today,* November 6, 1991, pp. 1–2C.
22. Ibid.
23. *USA Today,* October 18, 1991, p. 1C.
24. *USA Today,* June 16, 1992, p. 10C.
25. Ibid.
26. Clive Gammon, "A Day of Horror and Shame," *Sports Illustrated* (June 10, 1985), pp. 20–35.
27. Ibid., p. 24.
28. Gammon, "Thugs," p. 50. See also Clive Gammon, "Anger, Then Death," *Sports Illustrated* (April 24, 1989), pp. 24–25.
29. Ibid.
30. Ibid.
31. James A. Michener, *Sports in America* (New York: Random House, 1976), pp. 427–428.
32. Ibid., p. 429.

33. *USA Today,* July 29, 1991, p. 2C.
34. *USA Today,* April 21, 1992, p. 2C.

CHAPTER NINE

1. Roberts, p. 148.
2. *The Sporting News,* October 5, 1992, pp. 5–7S.
3. John Engstrom, "Muncey Killed in Crash," in Edward Ehre, ed., in *Best Sports Stories 1982* (New York: Dutton, 1982), pp. 148–51.
4. Hank Nuwer: personal interview with Fran Muncey.
5. Overfield, p. 449.
6. Seymour, p. 424.
7. Overfield, p. 449.
8. Roberts, p. 149.
9. *USA Today,* July 10, 1991, p. 6C. See also Whittingham, pp. 24–25.
10. *Ebony,* March 1990, p. 128.
11. McCallum, pp. 22, 142.
12. Ibid., p. 221.
13. Oates, p. 208; McCallum, 286–87.
14. Mike Meserole, ed., *The 1992 Sports Almanac* (Boston: Houghton Mifflin Company, 1992), p. 732.
15. Cosell, pp. 261–63.
16. *People,* November 23, 1987, pp. 122–23.
17. Ibid.
18. Bill Libby, *Great American Race Drivers* (New York: Cowles, 1970), pp. ix, 21.
19. Ibid., pp. 25–26.
20. Ibid., pp. 26–28.
21. Ibid., pp. 40–41.
22. Ibid., pp. 41–42.
23. Ibid., p. 160.
24. Ibid., pp. 160–62.

25. *USA Today,* August 14, 1992, p. 36.

26. Hinton, Ed. "Close Calls," *Sports Illustrated* (June 1, 1992), pp. 14–19.

27. Ibid.

28. Demak, Richard, " 'And Then She Just Disappeared,' " *Sports Illustrated* (June 16, 1986), pp. 18–19.

29. Ibid.

30. Gutman, p. 54.

31. William Nack, "The Razor's Edge," *Sports Illustrated* (May 6, 1991), pp. 52–64.

32. Demak, Richard. "Marfan Syndrome: A Silent Killer," *Sports Illustrated* (February 17, 1986), pp. 30–35.

33. Ibid., p. 30.

34. Ibid.

35. Ibid.

36. Hal Higdon, "Jim Fixx," in Dick Kaegel, *Best Sports Stories 1985* (St. Louis: The Sporting News, 1985), pp. 137–46.

37. Ibid., pp. 137–46.

38. *People,* March 19, 1990, pp. 43–44.

39. *USA Today,* March 31, 1992, p. 1C.

40. Gutman, pp. 64–65.

41. Serge Groussard, *The Blood of Israel* (New York: William Morrow, 1975), pp. 1–5.

42. Ibid.

BIBLIOGRAPHY

Aaron, Hank. *If I Had a Hammer*. New York: HarperCollins, 1991.

Boswell, Thomas. *How Life Imitates the World Series*. New York: Penguin, 1982.

Chronicle of Higher Education, The. January 1989 to December 1992 inclusive.

Cleveland, Charles B. *The Great Baseball Managers*. New York: Thomas Y. Crowell Company, 1950.

Cosell, Howard, with Shelby Whitfield. *What's Wrong with Sports*. New York: Pocket Books, 1991.

Creamer, Robert. *Stengel*. New York: Simon and Schuster, 1984.

Ehre, Edward, ed. *Best Sports Stories 1982*. New York: Dutton, 1982.

Groussard, Serge. *The Blood of Israel*. New York: William Morrow, 1975.

Gutman, Dan. *Baseball Babylon*. New York: Penguin, 1992.

Halberstam, David. *The Breaks of the Game*. New York: Alfred A. Knopf, 1981.

Hall, Donald, with Dock Ellis. *In the Country of Baseball*. New York: Fireside, 1976, 1989.

Hardwick, Elizabeth, ed. *The Best American Essays 1986*. New York: Ticknor & Fields, 1986.

Harris, David. *The League*. New York: Bantam, 1986.

Henderson, Thomas, and Peter Knobler. *Out of Control*. New York: G. P. Putnam's Sons, 1987.

Honig, Donald. *The Greatest First Basemen of All Time*. New York: Crown, 1988.

Kaegel, Dick. *Best Sports Stories 1985*. St. Louis: The Sporting News, 1985.

Lapchick, Richard, ed. *Fractured Focus: Sport as a Reflection of Society*. Lexington, Massachusetts: Lexington Books, 1986.

Libby, Bill. *Great American Race Drivers*. New York: Cowles, 1970.

Locke, Tates, and Bob Ibach. *Caught in the Net*. Champaign, Illinois: Leisure Press, 1982.

Marsh, Irving T., and Edward Ehre, ed. *Best Sports Stories 1960*. New York: Dutton, 1960.

Marsh, Irving T., and Edward Ehre, ed. *Thirty Years of Best Sports Stories*. New York: Dutton, 1975.

McCallum, John D. *The Encyclopedia of World Boxing Champions*. Radnor, Pennsylvania: Chilton, 1975.

Meserole, Mike, ed. *The 1992 Sports Almanac*. Boston: Houghton Mifflin, 1992.

Newsweek, May 5, 1980.

Nuwer, Hank. *Broken Pledges*. New York: Longstreet Press, 1990.

Okrent, Daniel, and Harris Lewine, ed. *The Ultimate Baseball Book*. Boston: Houghton Mifflin Company, 1979, 1981, 1984.

Rice, Russell. *Big Blue Machine*. Tomball, Texas: Strode Publishers, 1988.

Roberts, Michael. *Fans*. Washington: The New Republic Book Company, 1976.

Satellite Orbit, October 1986.

Seymour, Harold. *Baseball: The Golden Age.* New York: Oxford University Press, 1971.
The Sporting News, January 1985 to June 1992 inclusive.
Sports Illustrated, January 1985 to June 1992 inclusive.
Syracuse University Magazine, March 1990.
Thorn, John, and Pete Palmer, eds., *Total Baseball.* New York: Warner, 1989.
Tygiel, Jules. *Baseball's Great Experiment.* New York: Oxford University Press, 1983.
Walsh, Kenneth T. "Steroids Don't Pay Off." *U.S. News & World Report* (June 1, 1992), p. 63.
Ward, Arch, ed. *The Greatest Sports Stories from the Chicago Tribune.* New York: Barnes, 1953.
Whittingham, Richard. *Saturday Afternoon.* New York: Workman, 1985.
Wolff, Alexander, and Armen Keteyian. *Raw Recruits.* New York: Pocket Books, 1991.

INDEX

Italicized page numbers indicate photographs.

Aaron, Henry, 90, *91*, 92, 93, 95
Adams, Margo, 115, 116
Agents, 131–34
AIDS cases, 112–15
Alcohol/drug abuse, 65–84
  addiction, 81–84
  car accidents, 67, 78–79
  crusades against, 84
  death from, 65, 69, 78
  for pain relief, 75
  See also Steroid use
Alderman, Darrell, 78
Ali, Muhammad, 126, *127*, 155, 157
Allison, Clifford, 150–60
Alzado, Lyle, 51, *52*, 53–54
Anding, Peter, 121–22
Anifowoshe, Akeem, 155

Anson, Cap, 85, *86*
Ashe, Arthur, 112
Auto racing, 78, 156–60
Ayala, Tony, Jr., 107

Barkley, Charles, 98, 114
Baseball
  alcohol/drug abuse, 69–73, 78–82
  cheating, 126, 128–29
  deaths/injuries, 151–53, 162
  fan violence, 135–38, 139–40, 144, *145*, 146
  gambling, 15–24
  racism in, 85–94
  sex scandals, 107, 115–17, 120–21
Baseball, Little League, 123
Basketball, college
  alcohol/drug abuse, 73

187

Basketball, college (*cont.*)
  deaths/injuries, 165
  fan violence, 146
  gambling, 25–28
  racism in, 95–98, 101, 103
  recruiting scandals, 38–40, 41–42, 45–46
  sex scandals, 109–10, 112, 119–20
Basketball, professional
  alcohol/drug abuse, 73, 83–84
  fan violence, 140–41
  gambling, 28–31
  racism in, 95–98, 103
  sex scandals, 112–15
Baylor, Don, 93–94
Becker, Boris, 129–30
Belinsky, Bo, 116
Belle, Albert, 137–38
Bettenhausen, Tony, 159
Bias, Len, 65, *66,* 110
Black Sox scandal, 20–22
Blood doping, 62–63
Bloom, Lloyd, 131, *132,* 133
Body building, 54
Boggs, Wade, 115
Bonilla, Bobby, 140
Bostock, Lyman, 167
Boston racism, 87, 89
Bosworth, Brian, 57
Bowling, 83
Boxing
  cheating, 125–26
  deaths/injuries, 154–57
  fan violence, 146
  sex scandals, 104–06, 107

Burke, Glenn, 117
Burman, Bob, 157

Campanis, Al, 94
Carlos, John, 98–99
Casey, Hugh, 120
Chaikin, Tommy, 57–59
Chandler, A. B., 22, 89
Chapman, Ben, 89
Chapman, Ray, 151–52
Chase, Hal, 19–20, 21
Cheating, 123–34
  by agents, 131–34
  gambling and, 124–25
  history of, 124
Cicotte, Eddie, 20–22
Clay, Nigel, 109
Clinton, Nat, 95, *96,* 97
Cobb, Ty, 19, 137
Cosell, Howard, 16, 18, 101, 121, 154–55, 157
Courson, Steve, 55–56
Cycling, 62

Day, Todd, 45, 119–20
Deaths/injuries, 148–68
  drug-related, 65, 69, 78
  health status and, 162–65
  self-inflicted, 120–21, 160–62
  terrorists, 167
Dempsey, Jack, 126
Driesell, Lefty, 109–10
Drugs. *See* Alcohol/drug abuse; Steroid use
Duk Koo Kim, 155, *156*
Durocher, Leo, 22, 24
Dye, Pat, 125
Dykstra, Lenny, 78–79

Eckersley, Dennis, 81–82
Ellis, Dock, 71
Ervin, Leroy, 47

Fan violence, 135–47
  alcohol and, 144, 146
  autograph seekers, 147
  causes of, 138–39
  high school games, 141–42
  response to, 140–41
Fitzgerald, Jim, 157
Fixx, Jim, 163, *164*, 165
Football, college
  cheating, 124–25
  deaths/injuries, 153–54
  fan violence, 140
  gambling, 25
  racism in, 101
  recruiting scandals, 34–38, 40–41, 42
  sex scandals, 109
  steroid use, 56–59, 64
Football, professional
  alcohol/drug abuse, 67–69, 73–76
  deaths/injuries, 154
  gambling, 24–25
  racism in, 101
  sex scandals, 107, 110
  steroid use, 51–54, 55–56
Ford, Danny, 41
Fralic, Bill, 56
Fuhr, Grant, 76

Gambling, 15–33
  cheating and, 124–25
  compulsive, 16, 24–25
  legalization of, 32
  media and, 31–32
  point shaving, 25–28
  popularity of, 31
Garvey, Steve, 115–16
Gathers, Hank, 165, *166*
Giamatti, Bart, 15, 16, *17*, 18
Gibbs, Gary, 140
Gooden, Dwight, 70
Graf, Steffi, 130
Green, Dondré, 100
Green, Ted, 150
Gregory, George, 37
Griffin, Matt, 141
Griffith, Emile, 155

Hall, Galen, 42
Hall, Joe B., 38–39
Harding, Tonya, 168
Haskins, Clem, 97
Henderson, Thomas, 73, *74*, 75, 84
Hernandez, Keith, 70, 81
Hershberger, Willard, 162
Heston, Willie, 37
Hockey
  alcohol/drug abuse, 76–78
  fan violence, 144
  fighting, 148–50
Hogan, Hulk, 59
Homosexuality, 117–19
Horn, Ted, 159
Hornung, Paul, 24
Howe, Steve, 71, *72*
Hoyt, LaMarr, 70
Human growth hormones (HGH), 56, 58
Hunt, Carlos, 100

Hydroplane racing, 150–51
Hyman, Flo, 162

Injuries. See Deaths/injuries

Jackson, Reggie, 92
Jackson, Shoeless, Joe, 22
Johnson, Ben, 60, *61*, 62
Johnson, Earvin, 112, *113*, 114–15
Johnson, Jimmy, 44, 57, 140
Jordan, Chuck, 100
Jordan, Michael, 28, *29*, 30, 141

Karras, Alex, 24
Kekich, Mike, 116–17
Kemp, Jan, 47
Kerrigan, Nancy, 168
Kordic, John, 76, *77*, 78

Landis, Kenesaw M., 19, 22, *23*
Lapchick, Joe, 95, *96*, 97
Lipscomb, Eugene, 67, 69
Liston, Sonny, 126
Locke, Tates, 33, 121
Lockhart, Frank, 158
Long, Terry, 53, 56
Lucas, Jerry, 83–84

Mack, Connie, 129
Maki, Wayne, 150
Mancini, Ray, 155, *156*
Manley, Dexter, 48–49, 67, *68*
Manuel, Eric, 45–46

Maradona, Diego, 76
Marfan's syndrome, 162–63
Marichal, Juan, 153
Marinovich, Todd, 76
Martin, Billy, 79, *80*, 81, 117, 128
Mays, Carl, 151–52
Mays, Rex, 159
McLain, Gary, 73
McNabb, Edgar, 121
Moon, Warren, 101, *102*
Mourning, Alonzo, 101
Mullin, Chris, 83
Mullins, Roy Lee, 154
Muncey, Bill, 151
Murphy, Jimmy, 158–59

Niekro, Joe, 128
Nixon, Otis, 71, 73

Olson, Lisa, 110, *111*
Olympics, 134
  racism and, 98–99
  terrorist attack, 167
Ormsby, Kathy Love, 161

Pallone, Dave, 117, *118*
Paret, Benny, 155
Perry, Gaylord, 128
Person, Chuck, 41
Peterson, Fritz, 116–17
Portland, Renée, 119
Probert, Bob, 76

Racism, 85–103
  in high schools, 99–101
  ignorance and, 94–95
  protests against, 98–99, 100

reverse racism, 101, 103
"stacking" and, 101
Ramirez, Benji, 63
Rape, 104–09, 119–20
Recruiting scandals, 34–50
   admission standards and, 42–46
   black recruits and, 46–49
   media and, 38–39
   punishment for, 42
Reynolds, Joe Brett, 125
Rickey, Branch, 87, *88,* 89
Robertson, Torrie, 148, *149*
Robinson, Jackie, 87, *88,* 89–90
Rodman, Dennis, 103
Rogers, Don, 65
Rogers, Reggie, 67
Rose, Pete, *14,* 15–16, 18, 139–40
Roseboro, John, 153
Ross, Kevin, 48
Rothstein, Arnold, 21
Rozier, Mike, 133
Ruiz, Rosie, 130
Running, 130, 163–65
Rupp, Adolph, 25–26, 27, 97
Ruth, Babe, 13, 116, 137

Sabo, Chris, 147
Sanderson, Wimp, 110, 112
Schlichter, Art, 24–25
Schott, Marge, 95
Schwarzenegger, Arnold, 54, 64

Sex scandals, 104–122
   AIDS cases, 112–15
   coaches and, 121
   harassment, 109–12
   high school athletes and, 121–22
   homosexuality, 117–19
   media and, 116
   promiscuity, 114–17
   rapes, 104–9, 119–20
   victimization of athletes, 119–21
Sherrill, Jackie, 49–50
Smith, Robert, 46–47
Smith, Sonny, 41, 98
Smith, Tommie, 98–99
Snyder, Jimmy, 95
Soccer
   alcohol/drug abuse, 76
   cheating, 131
   fan violence, 142, *143,* 144
South Africa, 98
Sporting goods industry, 103
Stagg, Amos Alonzo, 124
Stahl, Chick, 121
Steinhagen, Ruth Ann, 135–36
Steroid use, 51–64
   addiction problem, 51
   dangers of, 53, 59
   in high schools, 63
   history of, 55
   laws on, 59
   tests for, 55, 56, 60
Strawberry, Darryl, 81, 103
Sutton, Eddie, 40, 45

191

Tarkanian, Jerry, 28
Tarpley, Roy, 73
Taylor, Lawrence, 76, 133
Tennis, 129–30
Thomas, Isiah, 103, 141
Thompson, John, 101, 103
Tilden, Bill, 119
Tomjanovich, Rudy, 160
Torrance, Gwen, 63
Track-and-field, 60–62, 161
Tyson, Mike, 104, *105*, 106

Vincent, Fay, 18, 32, 90
Volleyball, 162
Vukovich, Bill, 159

Waitkus, Eddie, 135–36
Walker, Welday, 85
Walters, Norby, 131, *132*, 133
Washington, Kermit, 160
Watts, Nancy, 110, 112
Weber, Pete, 83
Welch, Bob, 82
Welch, David, 141–42
Wiggins, Alan, 69–70
Willard, Jess, 126, 155
Worthy, James, 115
Wrestling, pro, 59–60

Yacht racing, 130–31
Yost, Fielding H., 35, *36*, 37–38